I Love You

Sandy —
This is My Love Story.
So... Just Love —
Carl Miller
2009

Booklocker.com, Inc. 2005

Author's website: www.corkmillner.com

First Edition: June 2005

Cover Photograph by Jilian West Millner

I Love You

A True Novel by

Cork Millner

I Love You

Dedicated to the memory of

Jilian West Millner

Mo ghra mo chroi

An ancient Celtic phrase, meaning,

My love my heart

A Place In Time

"*I feel as though I have known you forever,*" *she said.*
"*Have we been together somewhere in the past? As one heart
touches the other?*"

*He was too surprised to answer. It was a romantic notion.
Too farfetched for his pragmatic mind. He brushed his fingers
over her cheek and smiled.*

*She kissed his fingertips, the excitement rising in her voice.
"I've seen a vision of us in an earlier time, in Ireland, in the
1800s. It could be that some old love letters will show up.
Perhaps . . . " She breathed in deeply as if savoring the thought.
"A photograph."*

Then she added, "It is from our place in time."

Prologue

Down Cathedral

Down Patrick, Ireland

"Looks like a big slab of rock, not a tombstone," I said, looking down at the huge, flat stone embedded in a block of asphalt. I turned to my wife, Erin.

"You'd think Saint Patrick would have an imposing marker, something of marble," I added. Looking at the spires of Down Cathedral, I raised my arms dramatically to the overcast sky, which was as heavy and gray as the tombstone. "Why not a mammoth figure of the saint sculpted by Michelangelo, towering to the heavens!"

Erin pulled one arm down and kissed me on the nose. Her kiss and her smile were my reward for the absurd theatrics.

As I took a picture of the huge tombstone, our Irish guide, Rory, said, "During World War Two, American soldiers chipped away at the stone with their knives. Souvenirs of their visit to Ireland."

I noticed a slick spot where a sliver had recently been cut away. "Looks like people still take away souvenirs," I said.

Rory thrust both hands in the pockets of his wrinkled jacket. "Pilgrims from all over Ireland, and even America"—he grinned at Erin, his teeth brown from cigarette smoke—"come to Down Cathedral to honor our patron saint."

Except us, I thought.

We were here for another purpose. Erin and I had hired Rory, a red-haired, paunchy native of Down Patrick, as our tour guide. We wanted him to help us discover the burial place of her family ancestors. Erin knew from family records and letters that her mother had been born in Belfast, only forty miles north, and her grandmother was from Down Patrick. We were looking for a family lineage that could be traced back, perhaps, 200 years.

Earlier we'd visited two other churches, but the doors were locked. I wandered though the graveyards, looking at moldy tombstones set in the ground like jagged teeth. The leaden sky hung like a coffin cover over the scene of the dead. Our reward had been cold feet and soggy shoes.

Down Cathedral displayed more promise; the gravestones were old but more elaborate. Most of the graves had markers of varying sizes, some with sculpted figures, including one of an angel with folded wings. There were several large vaults, penned in by metal fences thickened with rust. The withered branches of the late autumn trees looked like the bones of dried skeletons. Rather apropos for a church graveyard, I thought.

I took Erin's hand and we followed Rory to the rear entrance of the cathedral. Erin wore white slacks and a black sweater. An Irish shawl, which she had bought at a linen factory in Belfast the day before, was draped over her shoulders. A wide-brimmed black hat fitted snugly on her head, not to shade her eyes, but to cover her head.

She had lost her hair.

The chemotherapy treatments had deprived her of her lustrous red hair ten months earlier. It had started to grow back into a pixie style that she liked, but on this cool day she had decided to wear one of her hats.

She stumbled on a cobblestone, and I clasped her arm, steadying her. Her forty-seven-year old body had withstood aggressive cancer treatments and the chemotherapy had taken its toll. Yet, her doctor had told us that, "Everything is significantly improved, and I couldn't have wished for better."

"Think this is the place?" I asked, trying to take her mind—and mine—off the cancer.

She looked up at me, her pale, jade-green eyes glowing. In a firm voice said, "I *know* it is."

Directly in our path as we entered the Cathedral stood a massive stone font. Erin dipped her fingers into the water and made the sign of the cross. I nodded my head in respect, as I always did when she took me to a Catholic Church. She loved the Spanish Mission in Santa Barbara, California and we often went there to Sunday mass, immersing ourselves in the historic church's peace and tranquility.

"The font, worn from millions of hands touching its rim, is made of granite," Rory said in his Irish accent, offering a little guidebook insight. "'Tis said to be the base of a stone cross dating a thousand years ago."

Erin looked around at the bare walls in the entryway. Seeing nothing, she continued into the nave of the cathedral. As she approached a stained glass window, Rory whispered, "The Saint Patrick window."

Erin nodded at the four figures of St. Patrick etched into the glass, then turned to look at the choir loft with its huge organ whose brass pipes almost reached to the vaulted ceiling. From her purse, she slipped out a folded letter, which was wrinkled from decades of handling. It was a letter that had been written to Erin's mother in November 1956 by a registrar of the cathedral. Erin's mother had marked these words:

3

We remember your mother well. She was the daughter of Mr. Henry Smyth, a much respected member of this town. She was brought up an Episcopal (Church of Ireland), was a good singer and a member of Down Cathedral Choir.

Erin eased onto a wooden bench and sighed, "My grand-mother sang in that choir loft. It's . . . as if I can almost see her."

I didn't say anything. Erin was clairvoyant. If she said she'd seen her grandmother, I'd believe her. She had revealed her psychic abilities to me on several occasions in the past.

She turned to Rory. "I need to talk to someone who works here."

Rory led us past the granite font to a back room with wood-paneled walls. The room smelled of dust, age, and forgotten records. A stocky woman, hips bulging in a plaid skirt that fell to her ankles, shook hands with Rory as he explained that we were looking for ancestral records.

"And the name of your ancestor?" the woman asked, a friendly smile creasing the deep lines around her mouth.

Erin handed the letter to her and pointed at the name, *Henry Smythe.*

"Ah, not to be a problem." So saying, the woman slid a huge leather-bound ledger, its edges frayed with time and use, from a shelf. With a grunt, she plopped it on a table. I watched with fascination as the woman leafed though the stiff pages, which crinkled like fall leaves. I noticed Erin studying the gold-framed pictures on the walls. I assumed they were drawings and photographs of past Bishops of the church. But I knew Erin was looking for something else—a photograph of *us.*

Lost in time . . .

I Love You

When we first began our romance five years earlier, Erin told me, "The photograph, the one I had a vision of, haunts my mind. I know it's of two people. The woman is a redhead, the man blonde with blue eyes, like you."

The next morning she shook me awake. I snuggled into her soft breast.

"Uh, uh, not now, lover." She pushed my head away. "What if the Irish redheaded girl was Catholic and the handsome, exciting man was Protestant? Like us. At that time the church would never allow them to marry. What if they were not destined to be together in *that* life, you know, because of the church. What if they made a vow to be together in *another* life! What if . . . my mind is racing."

She settled back down in the pillows. I stared at her. Even with her red hair in disarray, her smooth, line less face bereft of makeup, she was the loveliest creature on Earth. I watched as she closed her eyes as if to will her mind into another time. After a moment, she began to speak in a voice that I could only describe as ethereal:

"We will meet again—somewhere in time. "

"You have the prettiest eyes," the matronly churchwoman said as Erin turned from her study of the pictures on the wall.

I smiled, having been seduced countless times by those remarkable eyes. Erin's eyes were startling, a pale, luminous green like soft jade Looking into her eyes, I always had the feeling I was seeing deep within her soul.

"Ah, here we are," the churchwoman said, turning one more page of the old ledger. She pointed to two names in the book and read: "Margaret Smythe, died 1865, age forty-seven." She ran her finger down to the next line. "And this must be her

5

husband, Robert Smythe, died 1866, age sixty-eight. They died only a year apart."

Erin stared at me, and I could guess her thoughts. Margaret, who must have been her great-great grandmother, had been twenty years younger than her husband, Robert. And Erin was twenty years younger than *me*. She was forty-seven. I shrugged it off as mere coincidence and pulled my camera off my shoulder.

As I snapped a picture of the ledger page, Erin asked, "Are they buried in the Cathedral's graveyard?"

"Aye, they are," the woman said, pointing at the page with a chipped, red fingernail. "See, the register even lists a lot number."

"How do we find it?" I asked, clicking a final picture.

The woman closed the pages of the heavy book and brushed the dust off the cover. She went to a drawer and pulled out a linen scroll, browned with age, and unrolled it. The scroll showed a diagram of the graveyard. "Ah, here 'tis. Come, I'll show you." The woman laid the scroll on the open drawer. With a crook of her finger, she beckoned us to follow.

The sun had burned away the covering of clouds and the sky had turned a powder blue. I slipped on my sunglasses. The woman trudged past Saint Patrick's memorial stone, stumbling over one of the many lumps of thick, yellow grass, toward a tomb that stood about six feet high, enclosed by a rusty metal fence. "That's it," she said, wheezing, hands on her hips.

A tomb, I thought, impressed as I walked around it. There were only a few tombs in the graveyard, but this one, evidently Erin's family tomb, was, or at least had been, imposing. It appeared that no one had cared for it in decades. A growth of prickly holly obscured any sign of a marker.

Rory began to pull aside the holly at one end of the tomb. I helped, wincing as thorns pricked my skin. Finally, we uncovered a gray marble marker. Clearly engraved on it surface was the inscription:

MARGARET
DIED AT DOWNPATRICK JULY 1865,
AGE 47 YEARS
WIFE OF ROBERT SMYTHE,
DIED JULY 1866, AGE 68.

Erin stared at the uncovered inscription as I took pictures. With one hand on the railing to steady herself, she said, "My ancestors, my great-great grandfather and grandmother. I never really expected to find their tomb."

I pointed behind me. "And only twenty feet from Saint Patrick's stone. Your ancestors must have been rich."

"Undertakers," the churchwoman said, dusting off her plaid skirt. "The last Smythe died twenty, years ago. I read the obituaries. They were all undertakers."

I took a few more pictures, several with Erin standing by the tomb. Thanking the churchwoman, we walked away from the cathedral. I had my arm through Erin's when I felt her body go rigid, something I had seen before on our travels, usually when a ghost or apparition materialized. Eyes glazed, she said, "There's *something* here."

I said, "We found the tomb of your ancestors, the reason we came."

I could barely hear her voice as she whispered, "No, I mean *something* more."

A light breeze stirred the stark branches above us. Erin glanced upward and held her gaze until the breeze steadied. She shook her head. "It's . . . nothing. But for a moment I thought . . . "

I noticed a silent tear roll down Erin's cheek. She never cried aloud, even with the pain and anguish from the cancer, just the sad tears. She snuggled into my shoulder, and I could smell the floral scent of her perfume. "We'll find it," she said, her words muffled by my sweater. "We'll still find it somewhere—"

"—in time," I finished.

In the office, the churchwoman put the ledger back on the shelf and then walked to where the linen scroll was draped over the edge of the drawer. She wound the scroll around its stick and started to put it back when she noticed a thin object in the back recesses of the deep drawer, something she hadn't seen before. She reached in and pulled out what appeared to be a letter, one that had been sewn with thread in stitches to a stiff card. On the front of the yellowed envelope was the name:

Margaret

The woman looked around the room for a moment, then turned the envelope over. Printed on the card was a faded photograph of a man and woman. The woman was dressed in a long, full gown with ruffled bows, a flowered bonnet on her head. She was sitting, her cupid-bow lips pressed together in a slight smile, her attention on something in the far distance. The man, older than she, but handsome in a frock coat and cravat, stood next to her, hand resting on her shoulder. The photograph had been tinted in a few places: The man's wavy hair had been colored blonde and the woman's cheeks were pink. Her eyes . . .

The eyes had been tinted *jade green.*

Chapter 1

Clay's Story

Five Years Earlier

I shook her hand and read the Santa Barbara Writers Conference name tag pinned to her silk blouse:

ERIN HARDY
Santa Barbara, CA

I repeated her name, "Erin," then leaned toward her, catching a whiff of her delicate floral-scented perfume. I looked into her eyes, dusty green, intense. *The eyes of an Irish angel*, I thought. *Or the eyes of—*

"Are you a witch?" I asked, edging closer so the other student writers seated on either side of her wouldn't hear my question.

Startled, her eyes blinked, then flashed mysteriously. "Yes," she whispered.

My lecture notes slipped from my hand and fluttered to the carpet. I knelt in front of her to pick them up, noting the delicate curve of her leg. When I looked up, I could see her lips were creased into a smile.

"A good witch," she added.

9

I rose, embarrassed at the jarring crack of a knee bone, and stepped sideways to shake the hand of the next student writer, stating my name, Clay Mills. But my thoughts never left Erin Hardy.

She had entered my nonfiction writer's workshop a few minutes earlier. Her red hair, burnished by the light from the open doorway, radiated an amber haze throughout the room. She smiled tentatively in my direction then quickly took a seat on one of the plastic chairs near the fireplace, smoothing her short skirt under one thigh. It was a slow, sensual move, her fingers trailing past the hem of the material to brush her thigh encased in beige hose. She wore high heels in patterned brown and green tones that blended with her rust-colored skirt.

She was overdressed for the workshop. Perhaps she was going to lunch with a boyfriend after the workshop. Lover? I looked for a wedding ring, but her hand was hidden under a note pad.

Husband?

Strangely, the thought both depressed me and stirred my heart. She was the most attractive woman who had ever stepped into my writing workshop in the seventeen years I had been teaching nonfiction at the conference. Attractive? No, that wasn't good enough.

She was stunningly beautiful.

I sighed and looked at the other students who had gathered in the cottage living room on a circle on fold-up plastic chairs. Most of them were dressed casually, jeans, tennis shoes, a few long skirts and blouses, sandals. Although I had turned on the gas fireplace with it mottled ceramic logs, the room's temperature was a pleasant sixty-eight degrees. The fireplace, which emitted little heat, was decorative, an extra touch of ambiance to the workshop's living room atmosphere.

Table lamps and candle-shaped wall sconces added a soft touch to the illumination provided by a picture window. An expanse of grass and a brick sidewalk led to neighboring cottages. One student writer, notebook tucked under an arm, a Styrofoam cup of coffee in one hand, hurried along the uneven bricks, late for a 9:00 o'clock workshop. The annual conference was conducted at the Miramar Hotel, a sprawl of individual cottages, and a two-story building that had views of the beach. The setting created a warm, college campus atmosphere. The weeklong conference enrolled 350 wannabe writers each year.

Of the twenty-five student writers in my classroom, I guessed their ages ranged from twenty-five to seventy-five.

And Erin Hardy, my witch?

At a rusty sixty-two, I had lost my ability to accurately guess the age of a young woman. I glanced at Erin, mentally photographing her image. Her heart-shaped face and olive-tinted skin were unlined, the hands clear of thick veins, even wrinkles. She could be anywhere from thirty to thirty-six, certainly no older. A depressing thought.

Not that I was looking for an affair. During the years I had taught at the conference, there had been a few flirtations, but as a married man of almost forty years, I felt it was too late—or too ridiculous—for a mid-life crisis. Okay, senior-life crisis.

I took a deep breath—feeling a bit nervous with her gaze meeting mine—and told the gathered writers, "You are in a nonfiction writing class with six daily sessions. From this point on, I will call each of you a writer." I asked that they briefly introduce themselves by name and say a little about their writing project.

I was intrigued when Erin Hardy said she had begun a self-improvement book with the title, *Beauty Sleep – What*

Every Woman Should Know About Looking Divine. She added in a voice as mellow as morning fog, "My book shows how to sleep and grow young."

An older woman leaned toward Erin and said, "I'll buy a copy, quick!"

Erin didn't read from her book that day, which disappointed me, although I realized how difficult it is for novice writers to read from their work. When the class ended, I watched her rise from the chair, smooth the creases out of her skirt, and, with a slight hesitation, turn to the door. I tried to see her leave, but several students crowded around me with questions and I lost sight of her.

Erin returned to my class each day, finding a seat closer to me. On the fourth day she sat beside me, the scent of her perfume dusting me with lavender. She was coifed perfectly, her hair creating an amber halo around her face. Her mode of dress had evolved each day, never becoming too casual: slacks, sweater and high heels. I guessed her height to be a three or four inches over five feet.

Other than a brief hello, she never said anything. My witch—I still wondered why I had called her that (the green eyes, I suppose)—was a mystery woman.

At the end of the fourth class she did not move from my side. When the final questions of several students were answered and we were alone in the room, she asked if I would look at a few pages of her book.

I questioned: "Are you going to read in class?"

She hesitated. "I don't know if I should. I'm new at this. I'm not sure what the others might think." She quickly opened an envelope and slipped out several pages. She had created—or someone had—a color graphic on the title page, an illuminated starburst on a powder-blue background. As her fingertips passed over the cover, I watched the sculpted nails, peach hued, tracing a pattern around the words:

Beauty Sleep

"Did you do the graphic work?" I asked.

"My son taught me two years ago, when I first started using a computer."

Two years, I thought. I had been writing with a computer for twelve years, but had zero talent for creating artwork. And her son—how old was he? Sixteen at least. That could make her as old as . . . I vanquished the thought from my mind.

I noticed her staring at me, so I took the pages from her hand. "I would be pleased to read them."

After she left, I sank back into my chair, remembering the diamond wedding ring she wore on her finger. "Why hadn't I noticed before?" I asked myself aloud. She's probably been married for at least sixteen years.

Fool!

I slammed the door on the way out of the cottage.

That afternoon, I sat by the hotel's swimming pool, shaded by a palm tree, and began to read Erin's manuscript, expecting little, but hoping that this exotic woman had talent. As I read the first page, I began to sit up straighter. By the second page, my muscles tensed. At the end of the third page, I was stunned by the quality of her writing. She had painted a picture with words that was astonishing. I turned to the first page and began to read again:

> *A whisper of cool, fresh air brushed against my thirsty skin. The sweltering Egyptian sun had finally given way to the dark side of the day. The moon was full and bright and its light danced upon the waves of the sea that*

*surrounded the Temple of Sleep. The sacred water
called to me – ripples of delight washing against the
temple steps where I was sitting.*

I let the pages drop to my lap.

Midway through the conference a wine and cheese party
was scheduled to follow the afternoon workshops, a chance for
students to relax and get to know each other. The event was
held on the grass by one of the pools. Jug wine was served, so I
always brought an opened bottle of premium wine.

I saw Erin's red hair in the swirling mass of students and
shouldered my way to her. She was wearing a short skirt and a
green silk blouse. Without saying anything, I took her plastic
glass of chateaux cheapo, dumped it on the grass, and poured
from my bottle.

She sipped from my wine. "Umm, much better."

I toasted: "Never buy a wine with a sell-by date."

She laughed, a deep throaty laugh.

"Your name, Erin, it must be Irish. Besides, the red hair,
green eyes . . . " I was prying, but I wanted to know more about
her. "Does the name, Erin, mean anything?"

"It's a common Irish name. My mother was born in
Down Patrick; it's near Belfast. I've never been there, but I
know I'll go someday." She raised the wineglass to her lips.
"Thanks. This is really good."

"More where that came from." I touched her elbow.
"Let's go to a party."

She backed away a step. "I'm afraid I couldn't"

"It's safe." I leaned back, one hand to my heart. "*I'm*
safe."

She slanted one eye. "I'm not sure about that."

"Not to worry," I said, pointing to a second floor balcony overlooking the wine and cheese gathering. Several revelers were hanging over the railing waving at friends. "Shall we mingle with the party animals?"

"You'll protect me?" Erin asked, her tone mocking.

I held out my arm. "Your knight in shinning armor."

She touched my arm, sending electric currents through my body. "I think I'll call you my Beast."

"That makes you *my* Beauty." We were flirting, something I thought I'd forgotten how to do.

"Not the witch?"

"You're definitely, Beauty."

We climbed the steps, side-by-side. I didn't want her to think I was following her to catch a glimpse of her legs in the short skirt, although it was tempting. At the top, she coughed as she tried to catch her breath. I wondered why, but didn't say anything.

The apartment was jammed with students waving wine bottles, chattering in a steady din of voices. I introduced Erin to several of the partygoers, then led her to the balcony.

I eased next to her and poured more wine. We talked about the conference, Santa Barbara, nothing more personal. She didn't stay long, professing that she had to get back to her son, so I didn't say anything about her manuscript. I'd save my praise for the morning class.

She didn't return to my workshop the next day.

On Thursday, the last day of workshops, she showed up, dressed in the outfit she had worn the first day. I felt my body relax as if I had just slipped into a soothing bath.

"I'm sorry. I cheated on you," she said, her lips curving into a nervous smile. "I decided to go to another teacher's workshop."

I waited, my mind dancing with relief.

"I was wrong," she said, finding an empty chair to my right. "Did you get a chance to read my manuscript?"

"I want you to read in class today." I handed her the pages. "Let's see what the other writers think."

She appeared to visibly wilt. "You didn't like it."

"No, I didn't like it. " I paused. "I loved it."

Her eyes widened. "You're not just saying that?"

"You're an exceptionally fine writer."

In a tiny voice, she said, "Bless you."

When I called on Erin to read, she began haltingly, the foot of her crossed leg jerking nervously. By the second paragraph her voice steadied and the words came out in modulated tones.

> *"Many people came to the sleeping temple to be healed. Often they were chosen by the Gods, as I had been, or sometimes they were royalty blessed with riches that afforded them the luxury. The chance to dream in the temple was usually an honor only reserved for the elite. I was fortunate to have been called.*
>
> *"A fire burned in the center of the courtyard as attendants were busy preparing other candidates for entry into the temple. We were all to spend the night sleeping inside, waiting for a dream from the Gods that would either heal us of our illnesses, or initiate us into our destiny.*
>
> *"My attention floated to the water as I noticed a beautiful Goddess sitting on a large boulder nearby. Gently cupping the cool liquid into her hands, the enchantress caught my gaze and never let go of it. Her intoxicating eyes beckoned me to come forward and join her."*

16

I looked around the class to try and judge the reaction. The students were paying attention, concentrating might be a better word, and several brows were furrowed.

"Just then, I was startled by an approaching Priestess coming to assist me in taking off my clothing. Disrobed, I was greeted by two attendants carrying vessels. Each of them taking a hand, they guided me into the healing waters until it reached my waist. Taking turns, one by one, they dipped the vessels into the purifying water and poured the cool, sacred nectar over my body. The moonlight sparkled on my shoulders as each wash of water returned to the sea.
  "The Goddess vanished as swiftly as she had appeared as I was led back to the temple steps. Working hastily, the attendants dried my moisture-laden skin with soft towels. I was clothed in a silky white robe that clung eagerly against my breasts – the fabric folds falling lightly to the floor.
  "Arriving at the temple door, I was given a bowl of flowers and herbs to use as an offering. It was important to ask the Gods for permission to enter. On each side of the door was a lighted torch – the last light visible for the night.
  "The gate opened and I stepped in."

I noticed one man had his eyes closed. Asleep? Just listen to the words, I thought. Listen to the beauty of the words.

"The interior of the temple was dark and the floor was still warm from the heat of the day beneath my bare feet. A corridor ushered me deeper into the center

*of the temple. At its core were large pillars and columns
engraved with lotus patterns and messages from the
Gods – creating a circular opening into the night sky.
The stars were brilliant as if the gates of heaven had
been unlocked before my very eyes.*

*"Lying down on a soft, specially prepared bed,
more attendants joined me and anointed my feet and
forehead with fragrant oils. As they began to say
prayers and affirmations for my dreaming, I watched the
full moon rise to the top of the temple and was caressed
in its healing light.*

*"My eyelids became heavy while the soft
continuous droning of voices entranced me into the spell
of sleep . . ."*

Erin lowered the pages onto her lap, but didn't raise her
eyes to her audience. The room was silent.

I asked, "Opinions?"

Silence.

Finally, a rotund woman asked, "You sure you're not
writing fiction?"

Erin cleared her throat. "No, it's nonfiction."

"You mean, it happened to *you*," another woman chimed
in. "You went through all that stuff at the temple, the washing,
the purifying?"

"It was . . . a long time ago."

A long time ago? I wondered.

The large woman pressed on and asked the question that
had entered my mind. "You believe you were reincarnated?"

Erin looked uncomfortable and her crossed leg started to
jerk. Although I wanted to hear her answer, it was time for the
writing instructor in me to get into the act. "If we concentrate on

the writing style, we can see the images that the writer created. Did you feel you were in the scene?"

A young woman raised her hand. "I felt it was lyrical, like I was listening to poetry. I'd compare it to Marion Zimmer Bradley's *The Mists of Avalon.*"

Erin's eyes sparkled. "She's my favorite writer."

The man who appeared to have been asleep said, "You're writing is luminous. I closed my eyes when you read and let the words wash over me."

Erin's eyes glazed.

There were a few other comments, but other than the two rewarding remarks, the writers in the class didn't seem to understand the beauty of the words.

There were several other readers. During their readings Erin sat upright, looking attentive, but I knew she was thinking about the comments her classmates had given her. At the end, I wished the class well and told them I hoped to see them, or their books in the future.

Erin lingered behind.

Before I could say anything—I had decided to shy away from asking her about the reincarnation question, besides I was far too pragmatic to believe in the concept—she blurted, "I've been married one year."

She was a newlywed. I didn't need to tell her I was married. She'd surely noticed my gold band.

"I mean, I've been married before," she said, the words tumbling from her mouth. "My son's father was eighteen years older than me. I divorced eight years ago and recently remarried."

Why is she telling me this? I thought.

"Why am I telling you this?" Her face flushed as she began putting her papers and notes in a briefcase.

I had no answer, so I rose and shook her hand. "Goodbye Erin, my good witch."

She went to the door, pausing for a moment. Without turning back, she walked out.

I never thought I would to see her again.

Chapter 2

Erin's Story

It was June when I walked into the Santa Barbara Writers
Conference. I had paid the fee for the full week as a day
student. Many of the student writers were from out of town
and stayed at the old, seaside Miramar hotel. I lived five
minutes away. With a son and husband, I could hardly stay on
"campus," a term I heard several students use when checking in.

As I was studying the conference schedule of events, a
male student who was anxious to get my attention interrupted
me. And *not* about writing. He kept leaning into me and I could
smell his foul breath. I finally broke away when the insistent
man asked, "How old are you?"

Moving to a corner of the lobby, I again reviewed the
schedule of events, the speakers, and workshop leaders. I was
new to Santa Barbara and knew nothing about the instructors.
What workshop should I choose? Who could help me?

I was terribly nervous.

I had started writing one year earlier and really didn't
have any idea where I was going. I had never shared my
writing, except under the critical eye of my new spouse, which I
vowed *never* to do again.

I 'd had a diverse career. For ten years, when I was in
my late twenties and early thirties, I worked for several talent
agencies as a fashion swimsuit model. Oh, nothing big like
Sports Illustrated, but enough to keep my model's portfolio
filled with professional photographs and magazine tear sheets.

At five-foot, five-inches, I wasn't statuesque enough for the big magazines. Recently I'd appeared as the Spa Lady for Omni Hotels in an international ad campaign featured in national newspapers and magazines. I had been a host and co-host for radio shows, worked as a disc jockey, and had done several television commercials. But now, in my early forties, I had enough sense to realize that my modeling and acting careers were over.

My calling card noted the following:

Transformational journeys utilizing a blend of ancient healing techniques from a modern spiritual perspective
- ***Therapeutic Touch***
- ***Certified Hypnotherapist***
- ***Clairvoyant - Psychic Astrologer***
- ***Television – Radio – Public Appearances***

Yes, I was trained in all those areas and felt I was good at them, but I wanted something more creative—to be a writer. At the writers conference, I discovered that there were at least 300 novice writers who were living the fantasy of writing a bestseller.

I decided to take Clay Mills' workshop. I felt a little intimidated, not knowing much about his personality and patience with students.

So, that first day, the weather a bit humid, cool and balmy, I walked into the cottage where his class was held. There was a fire in the fireplace and students had already gathered. I sat quietly and patiently close to the fireplace.

Then he looked into my eyes and smiled and I knew I was in the right place. This man would be my teacher.

He began walking around the room shaking hands with each student, saying a few words. He did spend a bit of extra time with me, surprising me by asking, "Are you a witch?"

Why? Did he see something in my eyes? Did he realize I was clairvoyant, a psychic? It was the oddest question I'd ever been asked. Startled, I remember answering, "A good witch."

As he went back to his chair, I felt something shift inside of me, something tugging my heart. I suddenly felt sexy; a little bit of interest in his direction. I quickly re-examined my thoughts. After all, I *was* married. I had been married just over a year and my marriage was already having problems. After this conference, which my new husband hadn't wanted me to attend, we were due to go away for the Fourth of July weekend to Lake Arrowhead in the mountains near Los Angeles. I was hoping the trip would allow us to get to the heart of our problems.

I attended Clay's workshop—he jokingly told the students he didn't answer to his last name, or "Mr."—for the next four days, interested in the information he lectured on. I took notes and listened as other writers read their manuscripts. I didn't feel qualified to comment so I said nothing. I must have seemed like a mouse, a quiet one who'd slipped into the room under the door. I finally got up enough nerve to stay after class to give Clay several pages of my manuscript.

Nervously, I asked, "Would you mind reading some of my book?"

"Sure."

"You mean, *you'd* mind?"

He grinned. "Nope, as long as it's not 200 pages."

"Oh, no, only three pages." I quickly gave him the pages, mumbled, "Thanks," and backed out of the room.

Later that afternoon at the conference wine and cheese party, I was surprised when approached me and offered me some wine from the bottle he carried. When he invited me to a party, I shuddered a little. I couldn't attend a party with this man. He was married.

I was married.

He pointed to a balcony. *"That* party," he said. "Just a few students unwinding. Harmless, as I am."

That I wasn't too sure about.

At the party, I made my way to the balcony for air as several people were smoking, something my asthma couldn't handle. Clay and I did get to share wine on the balcony for a few moments. I wanted to talk about the pages I had given to him to read, but was terrified of his response, fearful he might say that I would never be a writer. Nervous, I explained that I needed to get home—for my son.

The next day I made a bad decision: I choose to go to another workshop, one taught by a woman. I thought that a woman's perspective on writing was what I needed. I also feared Clay's reaction to my writing.

Wrong.

I missed his teaching style, his humor, his smile, his warmth, and, yes, I missed him. Something inside of me was tingling.

When I went back to his class that last day, he seemed happy to see me. After I sat down, he leaned close to me and whispered, "My little green-eyed witch has been playing hooky."

What could I say? I nodded.

"Today, you read in class," he said firmly, jolting me. "Your name is first on my reading list. See." He pointed to my name, which was at the top of the paper, followed by half a dozen other names.

Oh, god, I thought, but said, "Yes."

I waited through his hour lecture. I don't remember a word he said, but was startled back to reality when I heard, "The first to read is Erin."

All eyes turned toward mousy me. I pressed the pages to my lap so they wouldn't rattle from my shaking fingers. I read, gaining confidence as the familiar words rolled off my tongue. By the end, I wished I had more to read.

Some of the comments from the students were a bit unusual. I was amazed at the response of the woman who compared my writing to Marion Zimmer Bradley, the one writer I wanted to emulate.

But the words I remember the deepest were from Clay. "You are an extraordinarily talented writer," he said.

After the conference was over, I sent my usual thank-you notes to everyone who had assisted me throughout the week. Clay was no exception. I was impressed enough to buy a special card, not the generic ones I kept in my desk. As I started to write a note on the card, I felt inclined to stop for a while and remember the odd feelings I'd had in his presence. Who was this man?

So I asked God.

I sat quietly in my usual prayer stance and reverently asked, "What is it about this man that tugs at my heart? Who is he?" I was surprised to receive an immediate answer. Sometimes God just sends thoughts. This time I heard him clearly, a deep voice ringing inside my head. "It is because he is your husband."

I thought, how absurd. That's impossible. Of course, it wouldn't be the first time I'd questioned His answers—I'm always challenging God.

I went on writing the thank-you note, but with God's answer in the back of my mind; I sent some *thoughts* in-between the lines. I hoped that someday, when the time was right, Clay would discover those hidden words. As I wrote, I said aloud, "If God is right, this man will."

Three months later I was on my way to divorce. I had begun to realize that every time I took a shower my husband would make a phone call. I could hear his muted voice over the spray of water. He would hang up when I came out. I checked redial and was greeted with an answer from a woman who hung up when I said my name.

When I confronted him, he confessed the identity of the woman: His old girlfriend.

My Irish temper flared. "You're still having an affair with her!"

He shrugged, apparently indifferent to my question. I saw the I-could-care-less look on his face and shouted, "We've only been married a year!"

"It's nothing," he insisted

"You bastard, you're screwing her behind my back."

I tried to slap him, but his strong arm grasped my wrist. My anger ebbed into sobs. Even though I'd realized months earlier that I wanted out of the marriage, I was devastated.

Divorce is an agony, no matter the circumstances. For three months I felt little more than numbness. I don't really remember much about the days from September to January. I took life one hour at a time, trying my best to solve the problems that arose. I spent those months healing financially. There were also problems to take care of for my son who would be graduating from high school in six months.

I spent Christmas with my family in Michigan, where I owned property. It was good to get away, have friendly voices around me.

When I returned to Santa Barbara in January, the dark cloud of dismay still hung over me. I had to get off my self-pity and begin writing again. But I was afraid. At that point I couldn't concentrate on much of anything for more than twenty minutes.

Once again, I prayed and asked God to show me a solution, to offer some light, some help. This time I didn't hear his voice, but a thought struck me: *Why not get the schedule for adult education and sign up for a writing class?*

Sure, God, get the schedule.

I felt like I was carrying on a conversation with myself. But where were the words coming from?

Oddly, when I picked up the schedule, I saw that there was one writing class starting the next day.

It was Clay Mills' class.

Chapter 3

Clay's Story

S hortly after the writers conference was over, I received a greeting card. The cover displayed a comic drawing of a turbaned swami on flying rug, saying,

This unworthy one can never hope to fully repay you
for your magnanimous gesture on one's behalf.
May you live for a thousand lifetimes
And feast upon
The fruits of paradise.

I opened the card and read the punch line:

Doesn't that sound better than, "Thanks a lot?"

I looked at the signature, saw it as from Erin Hardy, and hurriedly read the note:

Thank you so much for your encouragement and insight. It was a great pleasure working with you at the conference. I'm looking forward to seeing you again. God bless you for you kindness.
     Sincerely,
     Erin Hardy.

I reread the note several times, searching for lines that weren't written. I had to satisfy myself with the one that read: *I'm looking forward to seeing you again.*

Finally, I passed it off as a silly fantasy—either hers or mine—and forgot about it.

That is until that day in January when she walked into my life again.

Chapter 4

Erin's Story

I approached the class that morning with excitement and—once again—fear. Would I be able to pick up the pieces and start again? I hadn't written a word in my book for six months. Would I . . .

Then I saw Clay.

He was coming out of his classroom door, dressed in a navy sport coat and slacks. I didn't know if he'd remember me, but was inspired enough to give him a hello-again hug. He responded by holding me tighter than I'd expected. Hardly a "hello" hug.

"Erin," he said, staring into my eyes.

Well, at least he remembered my name, I thought, somewhat bemused by his warm greeting.

"And *Beauty Sleep*," he added.

My god, he remembers the name of my book.

He led me into the classroom. In the center was a long conference table. Seated around it were about twenty students. Chairs positioned against the wall on one side of the narrow room accommodated several students. I took one of the hard chairs against the wall as Clay began his lecture.

At the break, when we had a moment alone, I found it in my heart to tell him the truth. *Not too much*, I cautioned myself, *because you don't want to talk about your personal life, but just enough so he'll understand.*

"I've been through a divorce—" I paused when I saw the surprise in his eyes. When he didn't say anything, I added, "I haven't written in six months, and I need to start again."

He nodded.

"I need guidance, and support."

A grin curved the corners of his mouth. "I thought I'd lost my green-eyed witch."

"Your good witch."

His eyes flickered in amusement. "We'll see."

Yes! I tingled over that little innuendo, but I was glad I had showed up. If I hadn't, I don't know where I'd be today.

The weeks in his class were like a breath of fresh air for me. I found myself gaining momentum with each session, and I soon discovered my interest in writing again. I read from my manuscript in class and received positive responses. Clay took my new writing home with him, as he did each student's. He made corrections on the manuscript with a red pen, following up with in-class discussion.

When he joked that he was running out of red pens, one of the students brought him a packet of pens.

I started thanking him by e-mail.

We wrote to each other about the business of writing. I found a tender side to this man, one that became more and more apparent in his letters. I soon found myself confiding in him. Within a month, he had become a friend, a trusted one.

Then one day this e-mail came:

Would you like to go to lunch? To discuss writing. Strictly business.

Although I felt a bit nervous, I looked forward to the lunch. After class the following Thursday, I followed him in my BMW to the El Encanto Hotel, a beautiful spot, one that I had not yet seen. The hotel is located high in what is called the Santa Barbara Riviera with a view of the ocean and the Channel Islands. As we settled into our chairs in the dining room—he helped me with my chair—I felt warm and comfortable in his presence. It didn't take long to relax. Even though we mainly discussed writing, there were moments of personal inquisitiveness. Especially when he asked, "How old is your son?"

"He turned eighteen last December." Then I gave him the answer he wanted. "Two weeks ago, on March 14, I reached the creaky old age of forty-three."

I could see he was surprised. But I also saw he was pleased. I guessed him to be in his late fifties or early sixties, so our age differential was about fifteen or twenty years, maybe less.

Maybe just right, I silently amended.

He observed me a lot that day, sat back in his chair and watched my movements, my gestures. And thoughts, I realized. Finally, I said, "You're being terribly serious."

"I like serious."

"Why do you like serious?"

"Seriously . . . I don't know."

I laughed and felt snug and warm in his company. I didn't want the day to end. It felt so good to spend quality time, to have a fun, fulfilling conversation with a man I liked. I had been so immersed in my personal life and problems I'd forgotten what it was like to be alone with someone. Especially this handsome, talented, quiet man.

That day, as we left—he was such a gentleman—he paid the valet, helped me into my car and even gave me a little goodbye kiss on the cheek. As I drove off, waving outside the window with my fingers, I felt warm inside. Something was changing.

Thank you, God.

I decided to see if there was more to our relationship by using my expertise as an astrologer to find out how compatible we were. On my next e-mail, I told him I wanted to chart his horoscope and needed his birth dates and the hour he was born.

His reply surprised me:

Tell you my age! You don't know what "creaky" really is.
Okay, I'll give you the dates. But I'll lie.

He was afraid! I wrote back:

This is purely professional. You have to give me the exact dates.
Don't cheat or the whole thing is meaningless.

He didn't write. After two days, I asked:

At least tell me your sign.

He replied:

Slippery when wet.

I smiled and frowned at the same time, then sent him a foot-stomping e-mail:

Well?!!

The answer:

Yield?

My reply:

You had better!

That afternoon, this response came:

Okay, but once you know, this may be the end of a beautiful friendship.

He gave me the dates and when he listed his birthday as 25 December, I thought he might be fibbing. I wrote back:

Okay, Santa Claus, tell me the truth.

His answer:

Ho Ho Ho.

Then he added:
One year I got pajama tops for my birthday, the bottoms for Christmas.

I didn't think he would make that up, so I made his chart. He was, as I had surmised, twenty years older, which didn't bother me; my first husband had been eighteen years my senior. Besides, Clay looked ten years younger. Even more important, his chart told me what I'd already guessed—*we* were a perfect match.

When I told him, and said a little bit about my psychic abilities, he wrote back:

I should let you know that I spent twenty years—in what I call my "first life"—as a navy pilot landing on aircraft carriers. After 850 carrier landings, fifty at night, I quit because I was—terrified! (My mother always said I was a "slow learner.")

I had to laugh at that, but not at the next lines.

Because of my military training, I'm a pragmatic guy. This is evidently in conflict with your beliefs, but you should know how I feel. In my mind, anything that hints of the supernatural belongs in the shadowy realm of science fiction. I do not believe in astrology charts, tarot cards, Ouija boards, spiritual seances, channeling, and paranormal occurrences. I don't even like seaweed sandwiches.

That tirade angered me at first, even if the words were crouched in humor. These were my deep, lifelong beliefs. Besides, I wasn't exactly sure *how* he meant it. *Seaweed sandwiches?* Okay, so we weren't perfect for each other. I'd have to keep my philosophy to myself. Then I noticed how he had signed the letter:

Beast.

Beast? He mentioned the name at the conference, but he previously signed his e-mail, *Clay.* I wrote back, saying I thought the seaweed sandwich line was cute and asked why he'd signed the letter, *Beast.* He wrote back:

Simple. Now that you know my age and how I feel about things, I have become the Beast. If you notice the heading, it says, Beauty. From now on I'll think of us as Beauty and the Beast.

Beast.
Beauty.
A fairytale romance?

As the days turned into weeks, I found myself becoming more attracted to this man, his encouraging words, his sense of humor, a man with grace. One day in class, I thought, *He's very sensual. I wonder what he's like in bed?* I found myself picturing the two of us together. *Stop that, what are you doing?* But the thoughts and fantasies continued. Then the class ended. Ten weeks, once each Thursday, and it was over.

I gave him a bottle of Moet & Chandon champagne as a gift.

"I usually get an apple," he said, holding the bottle tightly, obviously pleased. He walked me to my black BMW convertible. As I opened the door, he leaned over to say goodbye with a gentle hug.

"Umm . . . I like you perfume."

He moved closer to me, and I felt waves of desire surge through my body. *What was that?* I thought.

I went home that day, totally unable to think of anything but my passionate feelings. I'd fallen in love with this man. I didn't know how or why, I only knew that something had happened deep inside me. My next e-mail explained it a little. I simply stated that when he smelled my perfume, *I felt quivering waves go through my body.* A big risk, I knew. My candor could end our friendship.

He responded with one word: *Quivering?*

In the next letter, he added this note:

Quivering is good. I look forward to the next time I press my nose to you neck. You see, I quaked. Okay, I trembled.
Pulsated?

And I knew we were fine.

Since his next writing class wouldn't start for another three weeks, our only form of communication was e-mail. He said he couldn't accept phone calls, nor could he call me because of his family life.

Family. Children. Marriage. I knew it was insane to become involved with a married man, knowing that it could only lead to heartbreak, but I so wanted to hear his voice, be close to him.

As the weeks progressed, I battled constantly about saying anything more to him. Our written conversations were still light, yet with a hint of interest. Then, one evening, I could no longer rein in my emotions. I wrote an e-mail, telling him that I thought I was falling in love. I stared at the words on the screen for a long time before I clicked, *Send.*

Strange, but as I write these words, I don't exactly remember his response—I wish I had saved all our e-mails in those early months—but I remember he was encouraging. Then he asked me out to lunch at an upscale restaurant near the beach.

We drove separately and as I got out of my car, he was by my side. That's when he surprised me with a single white rose, its petals edged in pink. My favorite rose color. At lunch that day he held my hand across the table and expressed his love for me. Not by shouting, "I love you!" but by saying, "Erin, I feel great affection for you, be that love, we will see."

After lunch, as he opened my car door, he asked me to wait a moment and returned to his car. He came back with a dozen white roses! I felt breathless; tears filled my eyes. I had never been treated so kindly, so lovingly, so romantically. He only gave me a quick kiss, the first one on the lips, and watched my eyes intently. I felt like springtime. Happy, feminine. Joyful.

He loves me!

And he's married.

Chapter 5

Beauty and the Beast

I was infatuated with Erin. Love? I loved to be with her, to talk to her, to touch her hand, to hear her laugh—to *look* at her. She was the most extraordinarily woman I had ever been close to. The shimmering red hair, the heart-shaped face, the throaty voice, the soft-green eyes, the perfectly painted fingernails, the sensual, well-shaped legs and body, which were accentuated by the fashionable clothes she wore.

She was also the most stimulating woman I had ever known, both intellectually and sensually. And I knew—as well as she —that what we felt for each other could only lead to a love affair.

I began to suffer deep feelings of guilt. I was cheating, sneaking around. Especially when I would meet Erin for lunch. I never knew who might be in the restaurant, a friend of mine, or worse, a friend of my wife's. Yet, there was something challenging in our secret rendezvous. Although I kept a wary eye on other tables in the restaurants, I had the feeling that I really didn't care if we were seen together. After all, it was still a flirtation, a taste of cotton candy. Infidelity, however, would be like sailing in a dark tunnel of love with no escape.

My marriage? I had been married for almost forty years to a woman I had known since I was a college student and she a sixteen-year-old high school girl. We had married when I was twenty-three, having served two years as a navy pilot. She had just turned twenty. My wife and I had traveled the world with my navy duties, raised two children, a daughter—who was soon to be married—and a son, both of whom had graduated from college.

It was a good marriage, perhaps a little old and frayed around the edges. Like all couples who live together for a long time, we had changed. She had become more commanding, in-control. I joked with her several times to stop taking aggressive training courses. I had become distant, unresponsive.

Love? I really didn't know what that word meant. My wife and I were *in* love, a comfortable, warm, I want to hold your hand kind of love. In all those years of marriage, I had never thought about leaving her. Yet, my infatuation with Erin was moving me in a direction I had never anticipated.

I continued addressing my e-mail to Erin as Beauty and signing them, Beast. In a bizarre way that made our relationship seem impersonal. We weren't really live, flesh-and-blood lovers. Instead, we were characters in a fairytale. What we were doing was not real. It was fantasy.

The e-mails continued.

Beauty,
I cherish the memory of that moment when I offered you the
white roses. In the sparkle that shone through the mist in your
eyes, I saw love. I have grown accustomed to your lovely face.
Nice legs, too.
Beast.

We went to the El Encanto for lunch again, this time sitting on the terrace, enjoying the distant view of the ocean. After lunch, I drove her up a winding road to little-known Franceschi Park. From this narrow shelf of land, we had a magnificent view of Santa Barbara. We got out of the car and I slipped behind her and put my arms around her waist. I could feel the nervousness in her body. I turned her around, and, for the first time, kissed her. Just one kiss, but it lingered.

Our flirtation had taken a new turn.

Erin wrote:

Beast,
God bless you for coming into my life, for inspiring my passion
for writing, for inspiring my passion. I am coming alive again.
It has been many years and I welcome it with open arms, but
know that I am in good hands. You are an angel.
Beauty

Beauty,
An angel? Moi?
Beast

Beast,
I have never met anyone who appreciates life like you do. I
marvel at the way you look at the birds, the sunsets and the
smallest most intricate delights of living. I didn't learn this
lesson until I cared for my mother when she had cancer and
died. She was 69. But, how lucky I am that all that has changed
for me. Life is so precious. It deserves attention. I am ready to
slow mine down now. I believe that when my son leaves for
college, I will streamline mine. The days of providing are over.
I can't wait to simplify and enjoy the few precious moments that
exist.

And you are the most important. Okay, I'm going to say it. I Love You.
Beauty

That was the first time Erin said she loved me. She had said, "I think I'm falling in love," but, "I love you?"

I agreed with her about life being precious, yet had a strange, unsettling feeling that she knew her life had *only* those "few precious moments." I wrote back:

Beauty,
One doesn't have to stop and count the roses, just slow down.
Make each moment last. As the song goes—the best is now. *I*
never thought the now *could be so wonderful. Yes, I love you.*
Beast

We found time to be together for an hour, this time alone on a secluded beach, under the threat of rain. I opened a bottle of wine; we tasted, then kissed. When we pulled apart, and we didn't do that for what seemed like forever, we caught our breaths as if we'd just been beached by the waves that crashed around us. Afterward, I wrote:

Beauty,
The gods (Aphrodite?) have been good to us, shielding us from
the rain, allowing us our space and a tiny bit of time to be
alone. Each moment I spend in your warm presence brings me
closer and closer to you. Your shoulders soft as pink velvet. I
hope the kiss I left there lingers. Love.
Beast

She replied:

Beast
Your kisses linger, the soft ones and the passionate ones. That
last kiss has inspired me to play my piano again. Tonight, I
selected "Somewhere in Time." It has a special place in my
heart as it was filmed in Michigan at my favorite hotel, the
Grand. But now it means more. I feel I have known you forever.
Sometimes I wonder: Did Elizabeth and Robert
Browning begin this way? Their correspondence has inspired
lovers throughout time. I wonder if the year 1845 would have
been more passionate for them had they had e-mail? Perhaps
letters are more romantic – they live forever.
A perfect portrait in time.
Beauty

In her next letter, Erin mentioned the Prom. Her son's
Senior Prom was a week away and she said she would be busy
with his tuxedo, flowers, not to mention the photos to be taken.
Then she said:

My son asked me a question I was unable to answer. He
quipped, "When you went to your prom was it as expensive as it
is today?" I thought for a while and suddenly realized I had
never been to a prom. Photographs in family albums show my
older sister in prom attire on the arm of her beau, but none of
me. Oh yes, I was frequently asked to the prom by admiring
young men, but was never able to say yes. Somehow, the money
was always there for my sister and her beautiful gowns, but
never for me. We had little money as I grew up and there were
always other necessities that took priority. My heart ached as I
watched other girls dress up like princess while I wore my
sister's hand-me-downs and rolled-up skirts.

Well, now as a woman, it saddens me that I have no memories of moments like my son is about to experience—I can only feel joy through him. I want so much to give him the memories he deserves, and I feel happy that I am capable of doing it for him. Life's precious moments are so few.

The good news is that Mom will have one glorious free night to herself. I believe I should plan something special that evening. Perhaps my own prom. My first prom dance.

Any Ideas?

Yes. I had an idea. One that made my heart beat faster, and, at the same time, beat in remorse. Our clandestine meetings had not been innocent, but now I was considering full-fledged adultery. Just thinking the word left a bitter taste in my mouth. It was a step I thought I'd never take. Yet my passion had overcome reason, so I plunged ahead.

My wife happened to be gone the weekend of Senior Prom night. I had two days free. I wrote:

Beauty,
Prom time! It's been a while, but I can still squire a beautiful woman to her first, personal, private prom. Will you join me for a two–day weekend? We will have that first dance.
My love,
Beast.

I almost didn't send the letter. I was asking for a commitment to stay with me two nights in a hotel. What if she said no?

Beast,
Yes! But what will I wear? I have to get dressed.
Beauty

Beauty,
Dressed? You have to get dressed?"
I have scheduled a lovely restaurant at 9:00 in the
evening, but first a glass of wine at the inn where we will be
staying. And there will be a sunset. Our first together.
Love, Beast

It was an enchanted weekend. We became lovers. I knew not what the future would bring. On Monday morning, I received this e-mail, written the night after I dropped Erin off at her home:

Dearest Beast,
I ache tonight. The pain is sweet nectar that pours over my
body. With all my heart and soul, I love thee. I love thee so
deeply.
Beauty.

The next morning, I answered:

Beauty,
I love thee but even more. Let me tell . . .
Memories – The whisper of a silk dress, a quiet dinner
by a fireplace that set fire to your amber hair and
ignited the jade in your eyes. Charles, our waiter, who
had to pay witness to a prom date who tried to ravish
her mate under the table, and how much her mate loved
it. A glass of cognac, the laughter, the sparkle of gaiety
in your eyes. A night of discovery, how we turned
together in sleep . . . But most of all, simply being alone
with my dearest Beauty.
Your Beast

She wrote back:

Beast,
Yes, my love, memories of this weekend linger like a sweet
perfume. I keep receiving flashes of moments that are too
precious to ever forget. I am still smelling the roses and
recollecting memories. It is sweet sleeping on them.
Love,
Beauty

Chapter 6

Lover's Leap

T he Santa Barbara Writers Conference started again and Erin attended my class each day. I told her, "You must be tired of my weary jokes."

She replied, "It's okay, I don't listen."

Startled, I said, "I see you taking notes."

She showed me her notebook's title: *Beauty Sleep.* "They're notes for my book." She smiled wickedly, leaned in and touched my thigh. "Angry with me, lover?"

"Never."

Although my duties as a teacher kept me busy during the week, Erin and I found time for a few late evening meetings. On several occasions we had a glass of wine at the hotel bar, listening to the music played by a jazz pianist, music we discovered we both loved. The dark bar was always crowded with student writers, noisily reliving the day.

One night, without Erin knowing, I asked the pianist to play, "Somewhere In Time." When she heard it, I could see her eyes mist in the dim light. She grasped my hand and mouthed the words, "I love you, Clay."

We listened until the tune ended, then, in a serious moment, she said, "I'll never be your mistress."

I took her hands in mine, holding tightly as if I released them we would break apart. "And I'll never make you cry."

When the conference ended, I wrote this e-mail:

Beauty,
I feel strangely at low ebb this morning. It is as though the tide
washed over me in the night and left me alone, stranded. A gray
and blue wave left me where I am.
    I felt so close to you last week. To have you near where I
could see your face each day, hear you laugh, see the love in
your eyes. I said that I would never make you cry real tears. Yet
I fear. That's how I feel this strange morning. When I am so
much in love.
    Beast

She answered:

Clay,
You must never be afraid of the glorious love we share. Love
always has its tears—of all varieties. I personally am rejoicing
that I am feeling many emotions – all inspired by your love. I
am feeling from my heart, an unfamiliar joy. Taking the risk of
becoming Dorothy's Tin Man is frightening, but it is those tears
that create all the heartfelt memories and inspire love to grow
deeper. It is normal to feel a letdown after such a big week,
especially when we were blessed to be near each other
constantly – a glimmer of what it will be like for us one day.
    You are my love, my shelter, my whole being. I love you,
my darling.
    Erin

It was the first time since we began e-mail addressing
each other as Beauty and Beast that she wrote, Clay, and signed,
Erin. *Reality? No*, I thought, *not yet.*
    Not yet!

I kept remembering what she said in the dim bar at the Miramar: "I will never be your mistress."

Either leave your wife, or . . .

That thought plagued me. How? Do I simply get out of bed one morning and say, "I'm leaving. I'm going to live with a younger woman. Thanks for all the good years. Tell the kids. Goodbye."

How?

Although my wife was a strong woman, I knew that my departure would be a devastating blow. As foolish and immature as it might sound, I did *not* want to hurt her.

Erin started keeping a journal, in which she mirrored my foreboding. For the first time she penned her feelings about my marriage. It was something we never discussed together, nor did we e-mail on the subject. Yet, it was on her mind. The first journal entry read.

I am content in knowing that this dear man loves me. When I am with him, I burst with love.

Today, I worry about him. He is making a difficult decision and is experiencing tremendous stress. I remember the turmoil involved in making similar decisions to leave a mate. I have changed my life many times. I know it can't be anything like the pressure he feels. It will require great courage for him to make the final commitment to us. He has so many memories and years invested in his marriage. I know that deep down inside he feels it is okay to make this change in his life.

Yet, I have a terrible feeling that he will think I am responsible for destroying his marriage. Can he handle that? Can I?

Part of me wants to feel responsible, but no, not here. It

*is my deepest feeling that we were meant to be together. Only
God knows a person's destiny. I can only pray to God's light to
care for all of us, his wife, children.*

*He is my first and only true love. I know this is the
beginning of the best years of my life. Time will tell the outcome
of my relationship with Clay. At this moment, I want to be his
wife more than life itself, yet I am not a patient woman.*

This time I must be.

The next day, she continued with this concern in her
journal:

*My mind couldn't help but delve into the memories of
Clay's life. He has had so many years—the joys, the tears—all
coming to a climax now. I can't help but question if it is right,
this love we share. I will never replace what he has shared with
his family. I worry how his children will accept me, although I
certainly don't expect them to. I hope his children will be
protective of him.*

*Who am I? Who am I to disrupt his life this way? Can he
really find joy with me? Or would there be more joy completing
the journey he is on with his family?*

*He must love me deeply to be willing to alter his life so
much. He is taking a risk, as I am, but one that will reward both
of us.*

*I know we have been together before. I have seen the
vision. We looked different—but the eyes. The eyes are always
the same. They show the soul.*

I love you, my dearest.

Her feelings of self-doubt echoed my thoughts. We were

both jumping off Lover's Leap, holding hands, not knowing whether we would be destroyed on the rocks below, or lifted away on a downy cloud to live our fantasy.

Chapter 7

Death of Beauty and the Beast

I realized that I didn't have the strength to tell my wife. I couldn't say to her, "It's over. I'm out of here!" I tried to express these feelings in an e-mail to Erin using our fantasy names:

> *Beauty,*
> *You once mentioned the "clatter in your head and heart." That describes my mind, too. I am desperately confused. This turmoil invades my mind and is ever present. I have lived two lives—as a pilot and now as a writer—through a long marriage, almost as long as you have years. Thrusting a sword into this marriage will cause a mortal wound. I simply don't know how my wife will react. I am searching for a way to ease the blow.*
> *Am I playing the part of a foolish, befuddled man? Am I the cliché of an older man who falls in love with a young woman only to see himself in a Dear Abby column, scorned. These thoughts trouble me.*
> *Beast*

In answer, Erin exploded in a rare burst of what I thought was Irish her temper.

Beast,
Time sure seems to have a habit of slipping away, doesn't it?
Now you need to do something to make me smile, because I am
no longer smiling today. I wonder in the deepest recesses of my
heart what is really going on. I can no longer pretend this
doesn't hurt. I am a patient woman with a soft heart. Now my
heart is breaking.
　　I love you more than life itself, my dearest, but the days
and nights are becoming more desolate. It is difficult to enjoy
the full moon or the sunset with a glass of wine while I picture
you at parties, events.
　　Love, Beauty

An hour later she wrote:

Beast,
I will always love you and continue to love, to support you, to
stand by your side. Know this, my love.
　　Beauty

These two letters stunned me. Yes, Erin had every
reason to be angry with me, but the first letter was so unlike her.
It was as if another person had stepped into her place and
composed the letter. Then the real Erin, my Erin, added that
second note. In a brooding mood, I answered:

Beauty,
　　I regret that you had to send a letter showing how
disappointed your are in me. I now know you have no
understanding of how terribly hard this is for me. My wife isn't
the reason for the end of my marriage. None of this is her fault.

Please do not be angry with me. I feel as if a small wedge has been thrust between us. That is no fault of yours. The blame rests with me.
I am so very tired.
Beast

She quickly replied:

Dearest Beast,
I am not angry with you and there isn't a wedge between us. I only needed to express my feelings. You are not at fault. It is a natural rite of passage we are going through. Please do not think I am disappointed in you. I am only frustrated and ready to be in your arms, to hear your voice, to love you for the rest of my days. I will be patient my love. I have to be. I could wait forever for you.
Beauty

She was right, of course. I had over reacted, yet the depth of frustration in her letter disturbed me. That night she wrote a passionate letter that was totally unlike any I had received before. This was a new Erin. A *different* Erin.

Beast,
I am hot for you tonight – beads of moisture, a glow glistening from my pores. I can smell your scent as if you are right next to me, highly erotic fragrance that makes my heart beat and my passion simmer. My skin feels soft, delicate and sensitive – anxious for your touch, your kisses, your desire.
I feel your fingers grace my skin ever so slightly, a tingle, a shiver waving throughout my body. Your kiss at the nape of my neck, gliding ever so slightly into the soft curve, the flower of my breast. My hips are starting to move – to undulate,

to flow in the rhythm of my passion. I can feel the swell, filling me with desire, the pulsing . . . Ah . . . To be one with you, to let my body explode in spasms of pleasure. Yes, your are with me tonight.

> *Love,*
> *Beauty*

I was intrigued enough by this erotic fantasy, to answer:

> *Beauty,*

Wow!

> *Beast*

Two days later, I received this letter:

> *Clay,*
> *I awakened from a bad dream last night and realized I was not going to call you Beast anymore. Although I love the Beast dearly, it is time to progress to the reality of our lives. Somehow, on some intricate, subconscious level, I believe the Beast is keeping us from moving forward – after all, does he ever really possess Beauty? It is time for Clay and Erin – for Clay and Erin there is a future.*
> *I love you.*
> *Erin*

She was right. The time for playacting was over. It was time to draw the curtain on Beauty and the Beast.

The next morning I told my wife I was leaving her.

Chapter 8

Erin and Clay

Erin's Journal

I was supposed to meet Clay today to talk about some financial problems we would have to solve, but while I was getting dressed, he called to cancel. And—
    Oh, my God!
He said he had told his wife he wanted out. He told her! After all these months, months that seemed to drag on and on, he told her—about me.
    "It will be a while before I get to see you," he added. "It's hard to say. I've got to settle a lot of things."
    Although he sounded calm on the phone, I could hear the tears in his voice. I can't imagine how he feels. My heart goes out to him and his family right now. He's going through one of the darkest days of his life.
    I've been praying all day - Please God, support him.
    I don't know what to do.

I don't know how I told my wife. It just happened. It was early morning, and we were having a quarrel . Not a knock-down-drag-out argument, but a husband and wife squabble. Then, suddenly, she asked, "Is there another woman?"

I paused for along time. Her question sounded like a line from a poorly written movie script, except this was real life.

She finally said, "There is."

"Yes," I answered.

She was surprisingly calm. Then her bitterness surfaced. "What do you want, an amicable separation served up on a silver platter?"

When I didn't answer, she sighed, the air gone out of her. "You want a divorce." It was not a question.

We talked for a while, neither of us raising our voices. Then, she said, "I agree to this separation, but only if we have a written agreement that you will not divorce me for a year."

I was stunned, but said yes to her terms. Perhaps she felt that an affair with a younger woman would burn itself out, that I'd come to my senses and we would resume our married life together. At that point, I would have agreed to anything. I told her I'd stay on for a week and get my personal things ready to go. By staying, all I did was make the situation worse. Certainly Erin was not happy.

Erin's Journal

I am heartsick today. I miss Clay - and I am upset. Yesterday we met at a little park by the ocean (he said his wife agreed to it). He shocked me when he said it would be a year before he filed for divorce. He never said he loved me and couldn't look at me directly in the eye for long. I am terrified to have gone this far and now see these responses in him.

I hope not, I hope he is just tired.

I wait and my stomach is in knots.

Ah, she was having misgiving, if not doubts. Yet, none of this I knew at the time. I did know that my life could be ruined if our new life together didn't succeed. I remember my son's girlfriend saying, "My father divorced my mother for a younger woman. It lasted two years."

A younger woman.

I was twenty years older than Erin. Although she never mentioned my age, even after doing the astrology chart, I wondered if she wished we were closer in age? I know I wanted to be younger. I never said the word, "old." I didn't feel old. I knew I looked ten years younger, but so did she. So, we were *still* twenty years apart! Would someone refer to her as my daughter? What could I give her, fifteen years? Ten? Maybe only five? I remembered a story about Humphery Bogart when he was considering marriage to Lauren Bacall, who was about thirty years his junior.

"How long will it last?" Bogart confided to a friend. "Maybe five years?"

The friend replied, "Yeah. But what a great five years."

And so the days passed with Erin and I preparing to leap into the abyss.

Chapter 9

Home is Where the Heart Is

Erin's Journal

*Today, I finally get to see Clay. He arrives at noon. Today is the day we will start our life together. As he walks out one door –
he enters another.*

Yet, I have become accustomed to my days alone. It will take some adjustment, having a man around the house again.
<u>I am doing the right thing!</u>

She continued her journal entry with scattered thoughts:

These past few weeks have been well spent – opening my life for him.

I am ready.

He will walk through the door proudly.

He will be sad and happy at the same time. I will do my best to help him.

Thank you, God, for the blessing of this beautiful man.

I am very nervous.

It was time for a reality check for both of us. Once the fairytale romance of Beauty and the Beast had been cast off, the enormity of what we had done began to settle heavily on our shoulders. Had I known what fragile ground we tread upon, I would have hastened back to my wife to beg her forgiveness.

Yet, when I walked though the door of Erin's home and into her arms, it seemed right. After all, we were desperately in love. (Or in "lust," as a male friend told me.)

The next morning we woke up in each other's arms, ready for the first day of a new beginning.

Erin's house—it would be weeks before I could say "our" home—was a three-bedroom ranch house on a quiet cul-de-sac. One bedroom was vacant because her son had moved out several months earlier to begin college. Erin used a front bedroom as an office. When she showed me the third bedroom to be used as my office, I saw that the window looked directly at a high, mottled wooden fence only six feet away.

I studied the graying redwood wall for a moment, and then said to Erin, "I could paste a scenic mural on it."

She smiled wanly, knowing I was disappointed. Then, her eyes brightened with mischief. "Let's paint it pink"

I hugged her and looked into her eyes. "Jade green."

We were in each other's arms constantly. Erin said, "I believe we're getting to know each other." Ten days after I moved in, Erin made one last entry into her journal:

Clay has been here a little over a week and we are settling in nicely. My nervousness is subsiding as we are gently getting used to each other. I know this transition is difficult for him, but he seems to be handling it well.
Moving forward today.

Catalina Island.

It had been my dream to travel with Erin, to take her to the many destinations I received assignments to write about. Catalina Island was just the place. I called an editor I knew and got an assignment to create a story on, "Catalina—The Island of Romance." Perfect. Then I contacted the Inn on Mt Ada, which had once been the Wrigley mansion and was now an elegant six-bedroom inn. The innkeepers agreed to comp a three-night stay, which was not bad as the room's price tag was over $500 a day.

Erin adored Catalina from the moment we boarded the ferry for the hour ride from Long Beach to the charming crescent-shaped city of Avalon. The snug harbor with bobbing sailboats welcomed us on our arrival. She was entranced with the view of Avalon from the terrace at the Inn on Mt. Ada. After dinner the first night we enjoyed a glass of port on the terrace, marveling at the lights of Avalon far below, which glowed like embers in a fire.

"I feel as if this Inn is our home," Erin said with a sigh.

I sipped from the glass of port and smiled. "Maybe we should tell the Wrigley's we're available for adoption."

We climbed the curving staircase to our second-floor room. As we passed a large studio photograph of Mrs. Ada Wrigley, Erin said, "She must have loved it here."

"I'll always remember her when I chew gum," I replied as I unlocked the door to our room, which had a ceramic tile labeling it *Bethany Glenn.* I clicked on the gas fireplace and pulled down the covers on the bed . . .

The last night we were there, as we stood on the terrace looking down on the lights of Avalon, Erin snuggled into my warm shoulder and said, "I want to be married here some day. On this terrace."

For the next month we continued settling into our shared life, learning the many things that our e-mail and brief romantic interludes had not revealed. There were a few moments when

Erin's Irish temper flared. On occasion this erupted into an argument.

I knew she had asthma, but at night it sounded like snoring. One time it became so loud I left the bed, grabbed a blanket, and slept on the couch. She was livid when she found me there. Swearing, she said she had bruises on her legs where I had kicked her in bed.

I said, "I don't want to fight," and tried to turn away from her, but she grabbed my arm, her eyes intense, face contorted. I walked away and left the house for a long walk.

When I returned, she had prepared breakfast. She never said a word about the one-sided argument. She gave me a hug and kissed me on the cheek as if nothing had happened. It was like she had changed into another person, then changed back.

Whenever I saw her temper flare, which was often, I brushed it off. We were still finding our way.

We took walks on the beach at sunset, basking in the joy of being together. We would take glasses of wine and toast to the orange sun as it flattened against horizon, then hold each other as the sky turned pink, then purple.

Yet, our time together wasn't purely idyllic.

I kept a constant lookout for my wife, walking her dog on the beach. One time when I did see her, I grabbed Erin's arm and hurried her off the beach. Erin didn't say anything, but I felt the anger in her tension-filled body.

We had a limited social life. I was reluctant to go out (the trip to Catalina had been like traveling to a sanctuary) fearing that we would be seen by one of my wife's friends. We were together, yet we were still hiding.

One encounter with a man and his wife, whom I knew from the social scene, proved painful. When I tried to introduce Erin, the woman grimaced angrily and turned her back. I could see the desperate, hurt look in Erin's eyes.

I constantly worried about the pain I'd caused my wife, especially after I received a note from her in which she sent fragments of poems she'd read in a book on *Lost Love*. Such lines as:

The forgetting is difficult, the remembering is worse.
I walk softly through life adding thickness each day.
The layers I have put around the pain of longing are
thin.
I found in you a home, your departure left me a
shelterless victim of a major disaster. I called the Red
Cross but they refused to send over a nurse.

At the end of that line, she added a note:
Funny, I thought, and drew a smiley face.
I cried.

Although I kept my own counsel and said nothing of my wife's communiqué, I'm sure Erin noticed my feelings of guilt and distress. To escape my dreary mindset, I obtained press tickets to the annual Vintner's Festival, which was held at a winery in the Santa Barbara County. I made reservations for two nights at a small hotel called the Chimney Sweep.

Erin adored The Chimney Sweep with its quaint cottages and what she called its enchanted gardens. "I'll use this scene in a book, someday," she said.

We enjoyed a candlelight dinner, complimented by a bottle of Chardonnay, and retired to our room. I went to sleep with a peaceful smile on my face.

"Brett! He's crying!"
The sharp sound of Erin's voice jarred me out of a deep sleep. I heard her click on the bedside lamp. Squinting, I checked my watch: 3:00 AM. I looked at Erin who sat rigid on

the bed, the sheets in disarray around her legs. Her eyes were wide, chest heaving.

"What . . . what's the matter?" I asked.

"It's Brett. Something's wrong. I heard him. He's in pain, some kind of trouble."

"It's just a bad dream," I said, soothing her arm with my hand.

She jerked away from me. "He's crying out for me!" She got out of bed. "I have to call him."

"Can't it wait until morning?"

She turned on me, eyes like green darts. "I told you, I'm psychic. I *heard* him." She pulled a jacket over her nightgown. "I'll use the cell phone in the car." Barefoot, she rushed out the door, slamming it behind her.

I sat in bed, feeling numb. I tried to go back to sleep, but my heart raced and my head throbbed. *What happened?* I asked myself over and over.

I heard the door open half an hour later. She mumbled, "My son's fine. I woke him up." She took off her jacket and placed the cell phone on the night table. She slipped into bed, turned her back to me, and mumbled, "Nothing's wrong."

Erin was mute at breakfast, not looking me in the eye. Finally, I said, "Look, as you know, I'm a pragmatic man. My mindset, which was developed in my military years is, like most military men, a 'show me' attitude. If I can't see it, I don't believe it." When she didn't reply, I went on. "I really don't know what went on last night. You said your son was in trouble, but when you called, nothing was wrong. I know you say you're psychic—"

"I don't want to talk about it," she said, her mouth a tight line.

Ah, what we learn in retrospect. I should have said, "I want to learn. I need to know all about your inner thoughts. Tell me about your clairvoyance, your psychic abilities. Teach me about astrology. Share this part of your life with me so I can understand. Let me in! Please, Erin."

Instead, I said nothing.

We drove to the Vintner's Festival. Over fifty local wineries had set up booths and poured wine while nearly as many restaurants served appetizers. I led Erin around to my favorite wineries, chatting with the winemakers, proudly introducing her to friends. Although she would say, "I'm pleased to meet you," that phrase was the extent of her conversation.

We drove home in silence. I kept thinking, *Why can't we talk this out? We have a problem, let's talk.* I almost smiled when I thought, *She's new age, I'm old age.* I began to think that blending our lives was impossible. I couldn't handle my guilt in leaving my wife, and Erin couldn't adjust to a full-time mate, a man who didn't understand her.

The next morning I went for a walk by myself, trying to sort out what had happened. But the fresh new day didn't offer new insights, nor did it bring any peace. I felt like Erin and I were two jigsaw pieces refusing to match—turn them this way and that way and they still didn't fit. The muscles in my back felt like they were tied in knots, my heart bursting through my chest. Something had to happen.

When I walked back into the house, Erin was standing in the center of the kitchen. She had that deadly look in her eyes. Before I could say anything, she said, "We should separate."

I breathed in long and deep and exhaled before saying, "Okay."

We only lasted three months, I thought.

She cocked her head and looked at me in a funny way, like she had expected more, a fight, an explanation.

But I was too tired. *So tired.* I felt like I had shed a great weight from my shoulders.

"Okay," I said once more as Beast turned away from Beauty.

Chapter 10

Boy Meets Girl, Boy Loses Girl, Boy . . .

"I want to find a life of my own."

My wife was sitting on the sofa in front of the blaze from an inviting fireplace, enjoying the warmth and cozy feeling, which I remembered so well. I looked around the living room. Nothing had changed, the furniture was the same, the collection of paintings on the walls were the ones we had bought during our travels throughout Europe at the duty stations I had served at as a navy pilot.

Just like home, I thought

"That's fine," I said, standing by the window that overlooked the polo field. "I'm looking for an apartment to rent. I already checked out a one-bedroom condo here at the polo field."

Only three minutes earlier, I had told her that Erin and I had split that morning. And I *had* checked out an unfurnished condo because I didn't want to come crawling back, begging to be let in. Besides, the idea of being alone, at least for a while, appealed to me. For the first time in six months I would be free of stress. I was in a giddy mood. But I carried it too far.

Pacing the room, I said, "You know, I've talked to three guys, all of whom went through a mid-life crisis: One of them left his wife for two years before coming back, another almost a year, and the last guy only made it for six months. I guess I hold

71

the record for short romances, three months." Then I looked at her. She wasn't smiling.

That's when she said, "I want to find a life of my own."

"Sure." I started backing to the door. "I'll let you know where I'm at, my phone number . . . "

That afternoon, I went back to Erin's house—it was no longer "our" home—and told her I had spoken to my wife. "I'm going apartment hunting," I said, looking into her eyes, which had softened from the morning fury. "I want to get out of here as soon as I can. I looked at a small, unfurnished condo but the rent is to steep for my present income. If I took it, I'd also have to buy furniture, a bed, sofa."

"Where will you look?" she asked. As Erin said this, I realized she was terribly tired. She looked dispirited, as though she'd just grasped the enormity of what had transpired during the last two days and what had happened that morning. I don't think she expected I'd try to jump back into my old life, nor look for an apartment the same day we broke up. I had no other options. Our great experiment at love and passion was in shambles.

Boy gets girl, boy loses girl . . . Roll the credits.

"I thought I'd go down to the beach," I said. There are hundreds of apartments, so I should be able to find a small furnished place in my price range."

"Can I go with you?" she asked. I could barely hear her.

"Well—"

"I want to." It was a plea.

Bad idea.

Ah, but the teary look on her face . . . "Why don't you follow me in your car."

"I'd like to ride with you."

Really bad idea.

"Okay."

We rode in silence. It was only a few minutes to the beach area, a trip we'd taken many times in the last three months to watch sunsets. Leaving Erin in the car, I checked out the most promising apartment complex, but there was a four-month waiting list. The next one was the same. I thought, *This is the middle of November, not the summer season, there must be something available.*

I drove to the next large group of apartments and got out of the car. "Can I come with you?" Erin asked in a sheepish voice and smiled weakly.

Careful . . .

Pause. "Sure."

We were shown to the second floor to a tiny furnished, kitchenette apartment with a tiny living room, a threadbare sofa, odorous bath, and bedroom with a lumpy mattress. The place was scruffy and smelled of stale tobacco smoke and the hundreds, probably thousands, of tourists who had passed through. Its one redeeming feature was a balcony that overlooked the ocean. I could hear the surf.

I asked the landlady. "How much?"

"Eight-hundred a month."

"Is it available now?" I was surprised when Erin asked this question, as she had been silent until then.

"Not 'till the middle of January."

"Then it won't work," I said, turning to go.

Erin cleared her throat. "I . . . I think you should take it."

I looked at her warily. "I wouldn't have a place to stay until January. That's over a month from now."

She looked at me steadily. "You can stay at our—*my* place until then."

I nodded, but thought, *Bad idea.*

Back at her house, I said, "I'll sleep on the couch."

Almost in slow motion, she moved her arm toward the bedroom. "The bed's bigger, king size."

I sighed. "Erin, we only been . . . 'divorced' "—I checked my watch—"for six hours and twenty-five minutes. I'd better sleep on the couch."

She nodded her head almost imperceptibly. "I'll get some sheets, pillows."

We slept apart, making our own breakfasts. I usually had a health drink, a blend of milk, or juice, and fruit; she liked fried ham, cheese, tomato and onion sandwiches. We didn't talk much, just ate then retired to our offices to work. A novel based on a screenplay of mine was going nowhere, but I continued to work on it to fill the empty hours. I had no idea what Erin was doing. Writing her novel? E-mailing friends, I assumed.

Each night I heard her crying in the bedroom.

One week after living this brother-sister act, as I slept restlessly, I felt something pressing on my blanket. In the dim light, I saw her sitting at the end of the couch near my feet. She reached up and grasped my hand. "I want you to come to bed with me."

I didn't say anything. I desperately wanted her, to feel that joy again, but now? We had broken up. Crashed and burned, as my navy aviator friends would say.

In a voice that was half tears, she said, "Please forgive me." Then she kissed me softly on the lips, a kiss that quickly became a passionate embrace. She led me to the bedroom . . .

The next morning at breakfast, she asked, "Are you still going to move into the apartment?"

"I signed a two-month lease."

She said, "We can cancel it. I'll pay the rent, or maybe sub-rent it."

"Erin, what we did last night was wonderful—"

"I want you to stay here with me, to be part of my life again."

"You're the one who kicked me out." I said the words steadily, trying not to get angry.

"It wasn't all my fault."

"I know."

"It's hard when you don't believe in me."

We were silent, afraid to say the next word. Finally, I said, "Erin, it isn't just your beliefs, that's something I can learn to understand. But your Irish temper—"

"I know. I have mood swings."

I wanted to say, *It's more than mood swings; it's like you can be two different people,* but I held my thoughts in check.

"I'll change."

"Can you?"

"Can *you*?" she responded.

"Can we?" we said in chorus.

We began sleeping in the same bed.

The next day I received a letter from my wife, in which she derided me for being so flippant when I last saw her. "You waltzed into my home all smiles and full of joy while I have been going through hell the last three months. Have you no concept of how I feel?" The letter went on in the same angry tone. I crumpled the paper and tossed it away.

Looking at it in the trashcan, I thought, *We had a small window of time to get back together. Now it appears that window has slammed shut.*

But, she was right. No matter what I did, it would be the wrong thing. And now I was back in bed with Erin. Just when I thought the pressure was off, the guilt feelings returned. I was cheating on my wife once again. I finally called her and told her

I was still in Erin's house, and that I had rented an apartment but couldn't move into it until mid-January. She asked one question. "Will you see me?"

I said, "Yes." A week later we had lunch, but she spent the hour holding back tears. My back tied up in knots. I was trying to put the puzzle pieces together again, but now there were three pieces that didn't fit.

In mid-December I received an assignment to do a story on the Delta Queen steamboat, which would cruise for a week on the Mississippi River over New Year's. It was an all expenses paid trip. What should I do? Call my wife? Tell Erin? Although we were sleeping together, we weren't really together. We both showed each other tenderness, but a wall existed between us. I no longer said, "I love you."

I shook my head, knowing I was doing the wrong thing as I made plans for Erin to be my companion on the Delta Queen, including two extra nights in New Orleans. She was ecstatic and danced around me like a little girl.

One last fling, I rationalized. Then, it's over. I'll go back to my wife—if she'll have me—send flowers, romance her, be part of her life again. Perhaps it was a charlatan's act to go on the trip with Erin, but that's what I decided, for good or bad.

On Christmas Eve, Erin asked me to attend Catholic Mass with her at the old Santa Barbara Mission. I joked, "My mother's a Kansas Methodist. She'll disown me."

"Please. I want you with me."

Erin had never said much about her Catholic faith, but I thought attending the service would be a good way to take pleasure in the holiday spirit.

The old mission was crowded on Christmas Eve. Erin and I were lucky to find an aisle where an extra row of had seats and been set up. The church was decked out in its festive finery with arrangements of flowers at the high altar, priests in gold vestments, and, lingering in the air like holiday perfume, the scent of incense.

Erin wore a pale-green dress that matched her jade-green eyes, high heels, and a gold necklace and earrings. She was stunning.

She grasped one of my hands in both of hers, and, as the service went on, I felt a surge of what I can only describe as overwhelming emotion, which coursed through my body like an electrical current. I looked at Erin and saw the silent tears on her cheeks. She mouthed the words, "I love you, Clay." I leaned toward her, my mouth to her ear, and said, "I love you, Erin." I felt a shudder go though her body, then she relaxed. We had made a connection—a renewal of our love for each other—at that moment in a Spanish Mission on Christmas Eve.

The Delta Queen

Four days before New Year's Eve, we were welcomed aboard the Delta Queen by a woman greeter dressed in an early 1900s costume. The Delta Queen is the only original, fully restored steam-powered paddle-wheeler plying the Mississippi.

Erin was enchanted with Tiffany-styled windows in the main lounge. Solid teak handrails, gleaming brass fittings, and colonial chairs added to the room's ambiance. The dramatic Grand Staircase, crowned by an elegant chandelier, reminded me of a time past where lady passengers would peacock down the staircase in their evening gowns.

Before the chimes for dinner rang, we watched the sunsets on the river, viewing them through a mist of water from the churning paddlewheel. Erin thought the glints of gold sparkling off the wake looked like a fantasy dragon's tail, curving with the slow turn of the boat.

On New Year's Eve she wore a red sequined dress with fringe that danced over her knees with each movement she made. Her dress was complimented by red sequined shoes, and sparkling, crescent earrings. We drank champagne until the wee hours.

Two days later, with the rhythm of the river still lively under our feet, it was time to depart the Delta Queen.

As I turned the room key to lock our door for the last time, I noticed that Erin was staring down at the lounge area between the Delta Queen's staterooms. Her back was rigid. I asked, "What's the matter?"

Without turning her head, she whispered, "I saw a ghost."

"Sure." Psychic powers or not, I was reluctant to believe she had seen a ghost.

She slowly turned toward me. "The ghost was there, on that settee." She nodded toward an old-fashioned settee with needlework floral patterns.

I narrowed my eyes in a half-hearted attempt to make a ghostly outline materialize. "Nope. Don't see a thing."

"It *was* a ghost, sitting on that settee like a normal person, short and stocky, with dark hair and big eyes and wearing a ruffled collar."

Easing past the settee, I pointed to an old, framed photograph of Captain 'Ma' Mary Greene. "It says that Mary was the first woman to earn both a Master's and a Pilot's license on steamboats." I squinted at Mary Green's photograph, noting that she appeared short and stocky with dark hair and large eyes. I cocked my head at Erin. "Sounds like a description of your ghost. Says she died in 1949. That's pretty long to be hanging around her boat."

Erin let her fingers trail over the carved back of the settee. "Mary has a strong desire to remain here," she said. "She loves it."

I noticed the chambermaid coming out of a room with a bundle of sheets in her arms and decided to settle this ghost problem. I asked her if she'd ever seen an apparition on the boat. Her answer surprised me.

"Sure," she said. "She keeps me company." The chambermaid tossed the sheets on an ever-growing stack of dirty linens. "I wish she'd help me with my work."

"Who?" I asked.

"Mrs. Green."

I glanced at Erin and noted the curl of a smile on her lips. "I saw her," Erin said.

The chambermaid nodded. "Isn't it nice that she let you know that she's here. I think spirits are temperamental."

Erin poked me in the ribs with an elbow. "They get frustrated when you don't see them, don't they, honey?"

I felt like I had entered the twilight zone. As I took Erin's arm and started to lead her away, I paused by the settee. Strange . . . there was a chilling breath of air.

Erin seemed to be floating on a cloud as we walked off the steamboat.

That was the first time I took Erin's beliefs, and her psychic abilities, seriously. I *believed* she saw a ghost. Even more, I began to believe in Erin.

We stayed in New Orleans' French Quarter for two additional nights, eating at fine restaurants, stolling by the shops and strip joints on Bourbon and Royal Streets. Once, to my surprise, Erin pulled my hand and led me into an adult store, captivated by the assortment of playtime toys, and sexy outfits. On a counter, I saw a small, glass-cased box, which held two brass balls the size of marbles.

"Ben Wa balls, " I said to Erin. "An oriental sex toy." I had learned something on my aircraft carrier travels to Japan and Hong Kong. I whispered in her ear, "It's said that if you put them in your vagina, the friction of the two brass balls offer exquisite delight."

In a loud voice, she cried, "I want them!" The clerk behind the counter didn't crack a smile.

I got her out of there before she bought any other exotic items.

The next morning we walked to Brennan's, a restaurant noted for Eggs Benedict and a Ramous Gin Fizz drink. It was only a two-block walk from our hotel and halfway en route Erin stopped, stiffened, and held tightly to my arm. At first I thought she'd seen another ghost.

"I'm losing one," she said, crossing her ankles and pressing her hand against her short skirt.

"What?"

"The Ben Wa balls. Before we left the hotel, I put them in and one's slipping out."

"You put . . .?"

She nodded.

"What are you going to do?" I asked. "We can hardly call a policeman. Although that would be a hell of a story to tell to his precinct buddies."

"Don't joke. I don't want a brass ball running down my leg between my panty hose."

"Can you make it to the restaurant?" I nodded to the Brennan's sign.

"I'll try." She pressed her legs together tightly and in a mincing walk, we made it to the restaurant. She disappeared into the ladies room.

I waited, and waited, telling the maitre 'd that my companion would be with me in a moment. I hoped.

Finally Erin came out, cheeks flushed. I looked at her quizzically. "What happened?"

She put her face close to mine. "I barely made it into a stall and slipped down my panty hose when it fell out and rolled under the stall's door and across the floor." She giggled. "I went out to get it and saw the ladies room attendant, a young black girl, chasing it across the floor on her hands and knees. She grabbed it and looked at me. I smiled inanely and told her it was a family heirloom."

The maitre 'd wondered what we were laughing about as he led us to a table.

One week after we got back to Santa Barbara, I moved into the beach apartment I'd rented. I promptly dubbed it the Cave.

Chapter 11

The Cave

I was alone. Well, not exactly alone. The "Cave" was open house to—whoever. That included Erin—and my wife. My problem was to insure their paths never crossed. I wanted my revitalized romance with Erin to continue, but expected that at some time in the near future my wife would ask me back into her life. When I first started the affair with Erin, I enjoyed the romance and excitement. Now the romantic affair had turned into a nerve-racking experience. As long as I was living in the cave, Erin and I were back to dating.

I was playing the juggler again.

I moved a few clothes into the Cave, dragged in my computer, and set it up on a small table. There was only a hard, fold-up chair, which I padded with pillows. Now I was ready to write. I felt that I had something to write about—a new novel.

A month earlier, Erin and I had seen the movie, *Shakespeare In Love*. I had completed my master's degree in Theatre Arts at the University of California in Santa Barbara with an emphasis in playwriting, and had studied Shakespeare's plays.

A scene in *Shakespeare in Love* captured my attention: Shakespeare is writing furiously on large parchment page, fingers blackened from dipping his pen in the inkwell. He scratches out a few words and writes corrections in the margin. As I watched the image on the *screen*, I wondered what a page of an original Shakespeare manuscript would be worth? I knew that only six signatures of Shakespeare existed and they were worth over a million dollars each. What would be the value of a complete manuscript! None had been discovered, not one fragment.

As we left the theatre, this thought besieged my mind: The value of an original manuscript would be priceless. Bill Gates, who paid over $30 million for the Leonardo da Vinci *Codex,* couldn't afford to buy it, and the Getty Museum Trust would have to empty its vaults.

I slapped my hands together. "Yes!"

Erin looked at me closely. "You eyes are afire. What's going on in that creative brain of yours?"

We continued walking. "Remember how I tell my student writers that you don't simply *get* an idea, you *recognize* an idea? Well, I just recognized one from a scene in the movie. I can write a mystery thriller like . . . like, *The Da Vinci Code*, a story of—yes!—a perilous and suspenseful pursuit to discover a lost manuscript of Shakespeare's."

"Better slow down," Erin said, "your face is flushed."

I took a deep breath. "What if the protagonist, a female, is clairvoyant and has a clue to the manuscripts existence? You're clairvoyant, you could help me with that, then—" But I had run down. I would start writing the story when I got to the Cave.

The Cave.

Erin hated it. We were back writing e-mails. A few weeks after I had moved in, she wrote*:*

You are a romantic and sensual cave man. But, I wonder if the time will ever come that you will take me out of your cave. My heart searches for an answer. My love for you is once again hidden behind closed doors. Will the day come that you will be proud to be seen with me in public again? Or will I always be a secret?

Three hours later, she wrote this e-mail:

I don't like dating. I have loved you with all my heart – given my life and self to you and now I am dating you. I visit you twice a week, make love to you, and have to accept that I will not see you for a few more days. I receive token hello calls, never knowing what you feel or are doing. For all I know you are seeing your wife.

The way I see it is, if a man really loves me he will move heaven and earth and climb mountains to have me. I am trying to be patient, but for what? I hear you say you don't know what you want, that you don't know what is going to happen. What about me???? Need I wait for another woman's decision to decide my own life? You must decide if you love her, or me. I cannot wait forever. It is possible to love both of us – but you must decide where you heart resides. The man waiting over the edge of the cliff must eventually decide to turn back or jump. You will be in turmoil until you decide to jump or not.

I love you with all my heart, but fear you are rapidly losing me. I am no longer a teenager with an aching heart. I am a 44-year old woman who is capable of loving you with every breath of my being, but I will not compromise myself. I know how very precious life is, having lost it many times. Time is relentless. It allows no mistakes. At this stage in your life, how can you question that? You either love me or you don't. Which is it?
     Erin

I had just been issued an ultimatum—electronically. I wanted to tell her: "This isn't all my fault! You are the one who has thrown my life into chaos. You are the one who could have, should have said, 'Let's sit down and calmly talk this out.' Instead, you said, bluntly, 'We should separate.' But it wasn't you. It was that *other person.*' Instead of saying these things, I wrote this letter:

> *Erin, my dear Erin,*
> *My cave is bleak.*
> *I have just been issued an ultimatum by the woman I love. You say you want a man who will move heaven and earth and climb mountains to have you. Yet, that is what I have done: I left my wife, a marriage of 40 years, and my family, my children, for you. I have jumped off the cliff for you and now, today, I fear I have leapt into blackness.*
> *Clay*

Was I punishing her? I knew she was right, I was treating her dismally. Our meetings at the Cave were clandestine. As I was agonizing over this, Erin wrote back:

> *I must be able to express my feelings. I want you more than life itself – but I am the one in blackness. This is because you do not tell me what's going on in your heart. I didn't write an ultimatum. I am only asking for you to let me in. My heart has opened wide and clear for you, I want nothing more than to spend the rest of my life in your arms. I see you feeling the glory of our love then setting it aside for a few days. I don't just love you on some days – I love you on all days – and my love prompts me to want to be with you. I am confused as to why you don't feel the same. You can, I can, move heaven and earth together if we only try.*
> *Love, Erin*

Less than an hour later, she added this note:

Dearest,
I can't seem to stop the tears. Forgive me if I hurt you with my
thoughts and my words. I have been sleeping 12-hour shifts –
didn't awaken until after nine this morning. I must be in
depression. I have watched you come and go these past two
weeks and it has apparently taken its toll on me. I will get
better, I promise.
I love you – Erin

I didn't want to hurt her or fight with her. But I could never be sure *who* I was fighting with. How could I base a relationship on guessing who would turn up next, let alone in a marriage? I didn't know what I wanted. Go back to my wife, try and live the same life as before? Stay with Erin?

Who did I *really* love?

I left the Cave for a walk on the beach to try and gather my thoughts. With the fresh air in my face, I realized she was right. We had never really tried to communicate. We hadn't peeled back the layers of what was inside each other. I decided to call her.

It was a mistake.

She was still angry, and I was back in a conversation I couldn't win. After repeating her ultimatum, her voice on fire, she screamed, "Damn you to hell!"

I told her, "Erin, I've got to hang up. I really don't know who I'm talking to."

Sick at heart, I took another walk on the beach. It was dark but a sliver of a moon smiled on me. I would wait and see what tomorrow would bring.

I went out the next morning for breakfast. When I returned to the Cave, I checked my phone messages. In an almost elfin voice, Erin left a series of message:

> "Hello sweetheart, this is Erin. It's about 9:30. I need to talk with you. I love you very much and I am just . . . just trying to understand. I need you to talk to me. After talking with you last night on the phone, I realized, that—"
> BEEP

(My telephone was only set for thirty seconds. She immediately dialed again):

> "After talking to you last night on the phone, I became very depressed and realized I didn't really understand why, when two people love each other so much, they are not together, and I became very frustrated. I want to talk to you. Please call me—"
> BEEP
> "What I wrote was not an ultimatum. I was simply following my heart and trying to understand where your heart is. I love you more than life itself. I would never do anything to hurt you. I think we need to help each other. We just need to talk and hold each other for a while and figure things out. Anyway, I love you."
> BEEP
> "Umm . . . forgive me. I would never, ever, intentionally hurt you. I'm just very sad. I love you more than life itself. I hope to hear from you sometime today. God bless you."
> BEEP

I thought that was her last message. Her voice had wavered toward the end; I could *feel* her sadness, see the tears, those silent tears. There was another message.

> "Well, surprise, it's me again. I'm going to Bates Road beach this evening at four-thirty and watch the sunset. If you'd like to join me there, I'd love to see you. So, anyway, the invitation's there. I'd love to share it with you."
> BEEP
> "I need to see you, sweetheart. Try to call me; that'd be really great. Anyway, I need you. I love you."
> BEEP

I played the messages several times that day and found myself smiling. Her voice was the Erin I knew, the Erin who was tender, sweet and loving.

My Erin.

At four-thirty I arrived at Bates Road beach. I could see her standing by the railing next to the stairs that led down to the beach. She was watching the fading sun, perhaps, thinking of our fading love. A breeze ruffled her hair, which was burnished by a golden sun. I didn't rush up to her. I stared, and told myself, *This is the girl I love, and will love forever.*

I walked up to her, shoes crunching on the footpath's gravel, a sound she couldn't hear because of the crashing waves below. I slipped my arms around her waist, caught the scent of her floral perfume, and whispered in her ear," "Don't be afraid, it's just a man who thinks you are the loveliest woman in the world." I turned her around. "I want to hold you in my arms and love you forever."

There were the tears in her eyes, but she smiled and pressed her head to my chest. I could feel her breathing deeply. I knew we were going to be all right.

Chapter 12

A Novel Life

*D*arling, word's can't express how thankful I am
to be loved by such a forgiving and kind man. I
have learned some important things this
weekend: 1) I will never again in my whole life let my
emotions over-run my common sense. 2) That it is OK to
trust love – real love stands strong. Ever since I was a
little girl, I was conditioned to believe that love would
always be illusive, that men simply do not stand by you.
I have learned by your actions and your words that is
not so. My love has grown deeper than ever as the result
of your understanding, loving support, and kindness.
God bless you.
I love you. Erin

I sat in the Cave on my pillow-stuffed chair staring at
this e-mail message on the monitor. Could she control her
emotions? Could I stand by her? Could I trust love? I smiled to
myself. Love? I had never really proposed marriage.

Shaking my head, I closed the e-mail and brought up the
first chapter of my novel, *To Be or Not To Be Shakespeare.* I
reread the first three pages. Trash. I had no idea where the story
was headed. I hadn't fleshed out my characters, nor had I been
to Shakespeare country in England.

Had never been to England . . .

I was still thinking about England the next evening in the Cave as Erin and I enjoyed a glass of Chardonnay. I sat beside her on the sofa, holding her half-completed manuscript, *Beauty Sleep,* in the palm of one hand. The book had run its course with agents; all of them had rejected it.

I said, "Erin, I really don't believe this is the book you want to write."

She nodded. "I fear this book. I know it's going nowhere."

"I don't feel you have your heart in it. You need something that will release your creativity. What you feel inside."

She took the manuscript from my hand and dropped it on the coffee table. "It's not what I want to write." She turned to me. "I know what I want to do—a novel. I've been thinking about it for a month. I have a title, it may not be the right one, but I want to call it *The Goddess Spot.* I've already done some research on-line. The book will be a fantasy and will take place in Glastonbury, England."

England.

As she said the word "England," I settled back into the sofa, thinking, *Maybe I'm the one who's psychic.*

Erin continued, the excitement in her voice rising. "I'll use a fictional character as my heroine, one I've named Caitrina McCain. There's Morgan le Fay, sister to King Arthur, and Merlin the Magician. It will be a search for everlasting life and the Holy Grail."

"A book you can write honestly, a book from the heart."

"Oh, yes!" She snuggled next to me on the couch, almost spilling my wine. "The novel will be based upon what I know. My experience is in the field of healing and spirituality. I

didn't tell you this before, but I'm a certified Hypnotherapist."
She looked at me guiltily. "I guess I should have told you."

I put my wine on the coffee table, reached for my
billfold and slipped out a folded card. On the front was the
embossed design of an angel's wing. "I found this on your desk
last week. I hope you don't mind my stealing it." I opened the
card and read:

Erin Hardy
***Transpersonal Journeys utilizing a blend of ancient
Healing techniques from a modern spiritual perspective.
Hypnotherapy - Past Life Regression - Therapeutic Touch
Astrological Consultations - Trans-Psychic/Clairvoyant***

"I guess there's a lot of stuff you haven't told me," I
said. "Perhaps if I share something from my past it will make it
easier. As you know, I had open-heart surgery, a single bypass,
eight years ago. I'm now healthier than I have ever been." I
took her hand and placed it on my chest where the scar was still
visible on my breastplate. "When I came out of the anesthetic, I
found myself in a hospital room, a space that was eerily white.
At the foot of my bed, I saw a woman dressed in a green blouse
and plaid skirt. She had red hair and dark brown eyes. She said,
'Hello. I came to see if you were all right.' "

Erin started to say something, but I stopped her. "Wait,
there's more. I dozed off from the anesthesia and when I awoke
a nurse was standing beside me. With a clear head, I asked if
she knew then name of the woman who'd been in my room
earlier. She told me that no one had been in my room. 'Visitors
aren't permitted immediately after surgery.' "

Erin was silent for a moment. "She . . . she was your
guardian angel."

"I know."

Erin threw her arms around me. "You saw an angel!"

I untangled myself from her embrace. "There, I've told you something I've never told anyone else. Perhaps you can tell me something about yourself, what you haven't told me before." I held up the card. "We never talked about any of this."

"I don't do any of that stuff anymore, not professionally." She swallowed as if something had caught in her throat. "I didn't want to tell you, because you're so—"

"Pragmatic?" I took her hands in mine. "Erin, I *am* open minded. You have wisdom I know nothing about, a treasure of knowledge. I want you to show me what you do with astrology."

"Maybe, sometime." Her voice was more like a squeak.

"Erin, I *believe* you can see ghosts."

Hesitantly, she said, "I am clairvoyant, I can see *things.* I see images, sometimes a strange light, at other times it's just a chill of air, the brush of a breeze, and I can *see* a person, like I did on the Delta Queen." She tipped her wine glass and drained it.

"You're supposed to sip wine, not inhale it," I said with a smile, pouring from the bottle.

"Guess I'm nervous. I really don't think I should tell you any more. You'd—"

I showed her the palm of my hand. "I can't tell if the lines in the palm of my hand reveal my future, but I am open-minded enough to let you show me how."

Erin blurted, "I have a gift."

I waited.

"I first knew when I was sixteen and I began seeing spirits. Uh-uh, don't get that befuddled look, not if you want to hear more. These . . . spirits would come to me, sit on my bed, pat me on the hand." Erin touched the back of my hand with a light brush of her fingers. "Like that, a feathery touch, more like the whisper of a breeze." She withdrew her fingers. "It gets a little strange now."

"This gift you say you have, it came from your Irish ancestry?"

"My mother was intuitive, not clairvoyant, but yes, it stems from her and my father's Irish background." She paused. "You *sure* you want me to go on?"

"I'm fascinated."

"I don't know whether to believe you, but here goes: My father visited me after his death." She pushed a few wisps of red hair away from her face, hesitant to continue. "It was totally dark in my bedroom and he tapped me on the shoulder, like he was trying to wake me. Then he sat on the edge of the bed. I could feel the indentation his body made on the blanket; his weight made the bed squeak. Then he touched my hand." Erin brushed my hand again. "It terrified me. No words were spoken, but I felt his presence." She took another sip of wine. "Pretty creepy, huh?"

I whistled the theme from the Twilight Zone, and wished I hadn't. Piqued, she didn't say anything until I urged, "Sorry. I sometimes react without thinking. I want you to go on."

She took a steadying breath. "I began seeing other spirits, ones that passed away, ones I could *talk* to. In Sedona, Arizona where I lived for two years, I was hired by the police to find missing people. I can locate them by going into a place that they'd been. I don't have to see a photograph, just look at the name."

"Smell a piece of the person's clothes, like a bloodhound?" I asked.

"I've had to hold things, such as clothing, so people believe I'm doing something. But I don't need props to *see* the person. It's like movie makers who see the complete film in images before its shot; reel after reel, they see the movie in their mind." She shrugged. "That's about it."

I said, "Can you conjure up the ghost of Shakespeare?"

"What?" She tilted her head inquisitively like a puppy.

"For my novel, which by the way, I have decided to title, *To Be or Not To Be Shakespeare.* Maybe not as good as your novel, *The Goddess Spot,* but—"

"Oh, I love it!' Then she frowned. "I can't materialize a person out of thin air. I'm not a wizard. I need to be where that person lived."

"Then let's go to England."

Her mouth dropped open. "You *mean* it."

"I don't have a magazine assignment to write a story on England, but it would be better to go without that pressure. Together we have enough money. We'd have to fly to London."

"Yes! I have a girlfriend in London, Elizabeth. She would put us up," she said, caught up in the idea. "Of course, she may live in a dumpy flat."

"Or a mansion!"

"Yes!" we said in chorus.

After a moment, I said, "From London we could rent a car and drive to Stratford-Upon Avon, Shakespeare country, then take you to Glastonbury, which is the site of your novel, or we could go there first."

"Oh, God, we have to do it!" Her eyes were dazzled with excitement.

On March fifteenth I moved back in Erin's house. When I called my wife and told her, her response was as I expected. She was furious.

"How can you move back in with that . . . that *person*?" she said over the telephone.

I wanted to reply, "You told me, you're trying to find your own life. So am I." But I said nothing.

Erin still went along when I taught my writing classes, taking notes for her novel. In one class, I made the mistake of joking about her being a fledgling writer. I glanced at her eyes, which were on fire, and knew I had made a mistake.

After class we drove in silence—she was in that mood again—to a cocktail lounge we liked to go to relax. As soon as our wine was served, she said, "Don't you ever do that to me again! I am a writer, a damn good one, and I have some pride. I expect you to support me!"

I mumbled an apology.

"Then, let's forget it," she said.

The next day at class I told the group that I wanted to amend what I had said about writer Erin Hardy. Then I read a note I had written:

"Author Erin Hardy is a painter of light with words. In her novel, *The Goddess Spot*, the prose appears on the page artfully composed to give the illusion of floating and fleeting light, not unlike a painting rendered by an impressionist artist—per- haps Renoir."

Erin loved me for it and said she would to use the quote in her book.

Whew.

In May, Erin stunned me by saying, "I want to sell the house."

I immediately became defensive. "Why?"

"I bought it four years ago when I first got to Santa Barbara and it has increased in value by at least a hundred thousand dollars. Besides, I don't think we want to live here anymore."

I knew what she was saying. We had few friends and were shunned by Santa Barbara society. Once, when I tried to introduce Erin to a close friend, the woman said, "My allegiance is with your wife." I was embarrassed and I knew the comment hurt Erin deeply.

I wanted to lash back at them, but Erin said, "It's okay, I know who I am." Yet, it never ceased to amaze me how cruel people could be. People—fortunately not the majority—seemed to love to make judgments about the personal lives of others. Especially, the life of a redheaded, green-eyed temptress alleged to have broken up a perfect marriage.

We knew we could never have a life surrounded by so much hatred. We needed to "get out of Dodge," to a new place where we could buy a little ranch and live idyllically for the rest of our lives. Erin was right. But to me a storybook ending seemed impossible.

"Where would we live?" I asked. I seemed to have been left out of the decision making process. I was angry but tried to be calm.

"I don't know, yet. Maybe Washington State. I have friends on the Olympic Peninsula who tell me they love it."

Washington State. It sounded like the end of the earth. Although I had traveled to many parts of the world in my navy career, I didn't want to move again. Erin was almost as nomadic as I had been. She was also younger and the move would be an adventure. For me it could be a disaster.

Erin put the house up for sale in June and it sold it within a month for the asking price. Without advising me, she rented a condo on the other side of town. When she announced what she'd done, I slumped in a chair and said, "I can't go."

I could see her eyes ignite once again. "You *must* go. I need you to pay half the rent. It's a nice place, a good area. All we have to do is move in our computers and clothes. We'll have a big garage sale, sell all the furniture except my mother's antiques, my piano and personal items, which I'll put in storage. The condo is an interim place before we find a home in Washington."

"Why didn't we make these decisions together?" I asked, realizing she was pressuring me to join her.

"Come with me," was all she said.

I felt I had no choice, so I packed up everything in my office, books, photographs, computer and clothes. After checking out the space in the condo, I decided there was room enough to put my personal items in the garage while she sent her furniture to storage. That way I had control. I could leave Erin by simply calling the movers. She realized what I was doing, but never said a word. It was as if she had decided on taking the gamble that I loved her enough to go with her to a place where we could live in harmony together.

Erin wanted to lease the condo through October. I told her I'd agree to a lease until the first of September, two months less than she wanted.

I was considering going back to my wife in September.

If she'd have me.

In August, we took the trip to England. I sensed that it would be the last time Erin and I would be together as a couple. I had a feeling Erin knew this too.

Chapter 13

Glastonbury, England

E rin had that look on her face again. Her body was rigid. Not from seeing a ghost, but from being sucked into the demolition derby of cars careening around us in London traffic. My concentration was intense: I was driving a Hertz rental car with a stick shift, steering from the right-hand side. I wasn't so concerned about having a bad accident, just a fender-bender that would impede our progress to the countryside.

So, hands gripping the wheel tightly, I plunged ahead into the swirling mass of moving metal and glass, each turn accompanied by the cacophony of horns, the smell of exhaust fumes and burning tire rubber. And sweat—mine.

Erin and I had arrived at Heathrow airport in London two days earlier. Bleary-eyed from jet lag, we were picked up by Erin's girlfriend, Elizabeth. She took us to her residence, warning us before hand that it was a bit unusual.

We drove into a courtyard that had seen better years. The garden sprouted with patches of unruly grass, a few flowers drooped helplessly from pots: more grass grew in the cracked cement than in the garden. The residence was neither a mansion nor a ramshackle house. It was funky. Elizabeth told us that in the early 1900s the place had been the estate home of a well-know artist.

She led us up two flights of narrow stairs, which, I found difficult to navigate with two heavy suitcases. I stumbled into a surprisingly large and comfortable living room. Through an arched picture window, I could see the decay in the backyard, more piled boxes, soaked from the London fog, and rusting appliances.

"Not quite the Ritz," I whispered to Erin, setting the suitcases down.

She gave me one of those "Shuss" looks.

We were introduced to the bathroom, a space the size of a bridge table. A miniscule clothes washer occupied one square of the room. The kitchen was even tinier, more like a phone booth. Dishes and pots were stacked on a quivering shelf. But our bedroom was more than adequate. We immediately flopped onto the queen-size bed and slept six hours.

Elizabeth, who was about the same age as Erin, was an attractive, gracious, and exuberant hostess. That evening she took us to a crowded, exclusive restaurant. When told there were no empty tables, she charged up to the maitre 'd and proclaimed, "I am Lady Forthsyte. You certainly must have a table for me and my friends, both of whom are world-famous writers from the colonies, America." Her tone of voice commanded the poor fellow to discover a table immediately. As we sat down, Elizabeth said, "Bloody piece of cake."

Erin and I knew we were in good hands.

After taking Erin on a two-day whirlwind tour of London and its exhaust cloaked subways, which aggravated her asthma, we plunged into the London traffic for our journey to Glastonbury. After several near misses playing dodge 'em around cars only a hair-breath away, we were suddenly disgorged from the London maelstrom onto a calm four-lane highway.

"Bloody piece of cake," I said to Erin, a told-you-I-could-do-it smirk on my lips. She was still too wide-eyed to reply.

Erin had suggested that en route to Glastonbury we look in on the circle of stones at Avenbury and the monoliths at Stonehenge. I had studied a road map for an hour before we started out, taking note of the country roads, which were colored brown and looked like a tangle of knotted ropes. They were not marked with numbers. Oh, well, I thought, the roads must have signs to guide drivers to the next town. I never should have gotten off the highway.

The country roads were excruciatingly narrow. Huge trucks bore down on us and passed so close you couldn't put a post card between the vehicles. Erin kept scooting toward me as if she wanted to crawl in my lap. After two hours of this, and losing our way several times, we arrived at Avenbury. We toured the ten-foot high stones (I had no idea of their meaning, but Erin was fascinated), then noticed a buzz of excitement. People were pointing to the slope of a field of golden hay.

"It's a crop circle!" Erin shouted.

From where we stood, about 200 yards away, we saw a perfect circle cut into the field of hay with geometric precision.

"I've never seen one before," Erin said.

"What do you think? Space invaders?" I asked. "Perhaps a lunatic farmer with a dancing tractor?"

Quite seriously, she said, "People from the past, from another place in space."

Sure.

We headed for Stonehenge. On the map it looked to be only a few rope curls away. We found it with relatively few wrong turns, and I began to feel like a native driver.

Erin and I walked around the jumble of huge stones set in a circle and took several photos. I sat down on the grass.

With a groan, I eased onto my back. I was tired. The tension-filled drive prompted a craving for an hour in steaming, bubbling Jacuzzi. As we departed Stonehenge, I guessed we had at least two hours to reach Glastonbury. It took a grueling five hours. By the time we found our accommodations—a private residence on the edge of Glastonbury—I was in a vegetative state.

"Wine," I told Erin as I got out of the car. I grasped my throat like a man parched from wandering across the Sahara desert. "I've got to have a *cool* glass of white wine. I feel like the burnt head of a match."

Erin hurried to the front door of the house. A matronly lady with gray spit curls and a flowered apron welcomed us inside her home, showing us into a comfortable living room filled with antique clocks and overstuffed couches. It smelled of old lace and a splash of whiskey.

"Aye, Americans, are ye?" she said in a discernable Irish accent. After we agreed to that, she showed us to a pleasant second floor bedroom with a brass four-poster bed that looked perfect for my old-maid aunt. I went back to the car and lugged the suitcases up the stairway, then rummaged through the one where I kept several bottles of wine. Of course, they were warm.

I trudged back down the stairs with the empty drinking glass I'd found by the bedside. Walking into the kitchen, I encountered a stubby, ruddy-faced gentleman who had a glass of dark liquid—whisky, I assumed—in his hand.

I held out my glass. "Could I get some ice?"

He looked at me, dumbfounded.

"You know, ice." I pointed to a refrigerator.

"Ah . . . never use it, lad." He took a slug of whiskey and wiped his lips with the back of his hand. "American are ye, now?"

I guess asking for ice classified me as an American. The landlady came in and the Irishman said to me, "The missus, she'll get some ice for ye."

"It's ice ye want?" She shook her head. "Oh, my." She opened the small refrigerator, reached into the tiny freezer and proudly came up with one ice cube, which she plunked in my glass.

In the room, I poured white wine over the single cube and watched the ice sizzle and vanish. I poured half a glass of *iced* wine for Erin and we toasted our safe arrival in Glastonbury.

The next day, after a breakfast of orange juice, eggs, potatoes, bangers (sausages), jam, toast and coffee, cooked by our Irish landlady, we toured the town. The first thing we noted was the unusual people in costume. At least I assumed they were in costume. We passed maidens who looked like refugees from King Arthur's era. I counted five men attired in Merlin the Magician outfits.

"Tomorrow is Halloween," Erin said, "but some of them probably dress like Merlin all the time."

I thought they were just weird, lost in a time warp.

Erin grabbed my arm. "Let's climb to the top of The Tor."

We rounded the corner and could see The Tor, a large oval shaped hill with terraces leading to the top. An old church tower was perched on the peak of the hill. This was why Erin had come to Glastonbury. The Tor was the core of her novel, *The Goddess Spot*.

"The labyrinth," Erin said, sounding awestruck. "A passage to the Otherworld."

We climbed to the top, a heart-pounding journey. Erin pulled out an inhaler for her asthma and sucked in deeply.

From the top of the hill, we took in the magnificent view of the village below. We could hear the whir of traffic and the buzz of electrical wires. I sat on a stone bench next to the Tower of St. Michael, all that was left of a medieval church built in the 14th Century.

Erin sat beside to me, breathing more easily now. "The Tor is, and has been to many people, a place of magic, the focus of legend and superstition. There's a theory that the terraces form a three-dimensional maze. One story goes that there's a hollow space inside. And a legend, perhaps ancient, records that the hill has a secret entrance to the Otherworld. This is where my novel takes place, here on The Tor—and in the Otherworld."

We lingered for an hour as Erin took notes, then she was ready to go. "We'll come back tomorrow, before sunrise."

"What time's sunrise?" I asked.

"About six in the morning. We'll have to start an hour before that."

I groaned when I got out of bed the next morning. It was dark outside! But I knew it was important to Erin. She had to see sunrise on The Tor.

It was damp and cold as we made the climb in the dark, the only light to show us the way came from the dim glow of the village's street lamps far below. We'd unwisely dressed in shorts and tee shirts—the previous day had had been hot—but I had brought along a car blanket and draped it around Erin's shoulders. About fifty feet below the crest of the hill, she paused.

"The sun should rise just to the side of the tower," she said. "We can see it best from here."

I could see the shadowy outline of the medieval church tower as the sky began to gray. We huddled in the blanket on the wet grass, shivered, and waited. A family of rabbits munched their way through clumps of grass, which reminded me we'd been up too early for an English feast. My stomach growled, and I pretended I could smell coffee, eggs, bacon—

"There, look," Erin said in a hushed voice. She pointed to the tower.

Just around the stone edge of the tower, a sliver of silver began to emerge, then slowly widen into a circle. The thick gray of morning made the sun appear ethereal, a radiant disc that seemed more suited to a distant planet. I stared at it in awe, then snapped a couple pictures, knowing I could never capture the grandeur of what my eyes recorded.

In my heart, I thanked Erin for our journey to this mystical place.

In her manuscript, *The Goddess Spot*, Erin wrote of the experience, as seen through the eyes, of her character, Caitrina:

> *Caitrina noted that The Tor looked like an island surrounded by a Lake of Wonder. She mused that King Arthur and his half-sister, the wicked, raven-like witch Morgan le Fey, had seen this same scene. For a moment, she thought she saw the witch, Morgan, walking among the apple trees, but then a silver mist drenched the valley, filling in the hollows and rising like a tide. It hid everything from sight except for the tops of the trees and a few scattered knolls.*
>
> *The sunrise seemed to be taking forever. With a feeling of boredom and disappointment, Caitrina kicked an empty beer bottle aside that had been left by celebrating tourists the night before.*
>
> *Some magic . . . she thought.*

Yet, it was magic to be in this mystic place with Erin.

Chapter 14

Stratford-Upon-Avon

"I can't believe it," the woman in front of us said to her two companions as she stepped on a flagstone in Shakespeare's birthplace. "I am walking on the same floor where Shakespeare once walked."

Erin coughed, uncomfortable in dry and dank air. I felt as if the oxygen had been sucked out of the house by the horde of visitors who crowded through the narrow passageways and small rooms. I knew Erin didn't feel any *energy* from the past, no vision of Shakespeare. Only lifeless air.

"I've got to get out of here," she said, cupping her hand over her mouth.

To our dismay, we had to pass through room after room of gift shops to reach the exit. On display were quills with multi-colored ostrich plumes, maps, postcards, Shakespeare coloring books, even velvet paintings of the Bard.

"Bardolatry," I said as we once again stood in front of the Shakespeare's birthplace. Erin breathed deeply of the fresh air and looked around at the people staring in awe at the house.

"I believe this house was once a tavern called the Maidenhead," I said. Before she could respond, I added, "A local wag once said the tavern's sign was the only maidenhead in Stratford."

She put her arm through mine and snuggled into my shoulder.

We had been walking for about an hour in Stratford-Upon-Avon. From Glastonbury—about two hours away—the drive had been comparatively easy. I only got lost twice.

We had pulled up in front of the Shakespeare Hotel, which was reputed to be 400-years old. Our room, with its dark wood and creaking floor, was charming. We had sandwiches and a beer in the hotel bar, then started our walk. My plan was to tour all the places Shakespeare had been in hopes that Erin might actually see his ghost.

I believed she could.

"I'd like to see Anne Hathaway's cottage," I said, leading Erin away from Shakespeare's house. "Anne married Shakespeare in an Elizabethan version of a shotgun wedding—she was pregnant—and seven years older than him."

We retraced the steps young William Shakespeare would have taken from his father's home on Hendley Street, which we had just visited, to Anne Hathaway's cottage, a mile walk on a narrow path. As we strolled hand in hand under the shade of an umbrella of trees, Erin said, "He was going to see a pretty girl. He wasn't Shakespeare, he was just—"

"A horny teenager?"

She elbowed me in the side. "Okay, I'll amend my statement: He was a horny teenager in love." She paused and listened to the rustle of the leaves in the trees. "I can almost *feel* his anticipation."

After paying an entry fee at Anne Hathaway's cottage, we entered the thatched-roofed home.

In the kitchen, a male guide in a baggy tweed sport coat, an Irish cap pulled tightly to his brows, lectured to a group of tourists. "This is the 'courting-settee,' a stiff-backed wooden bench on which young William Shakespeare and Anne were said to have sat together under the watchful eyes of her parents." He spoke in a cultured accent that contained a hint of boredom, no doubt from repeating the lines too many times. "Although the house is referred to as Anne Hathaway's cottage, the young lovers never lived here as a married couple. After their marriage they stayed with his parents."

I watched Erin closely as she looked around, being careful not to disrupt her thoughts. Then, she shook her head. We left the house few minutes later.

"Where to now?" she asked.

I opened my guide map. "Looks like a mile walk back to town, then to Holy Trinity Church where Shakespeare is entombed. You up to it?"

"I'm the one who made you climb The Tor—twice. I owe you." She clasped my hand tightly. "Let's go."

A double line of trees arched over the wide gravel pathway that led to the entrance of Holy Trinity Church. We paused in the dappled shade and looked at the church's graveyard where great stone slabs used as grave markers stood crookedly on the grass like jagged teeth. Blackened with dry rot, the inscriptions were almost impossible to read, but enough could be deciphered to see that most of the stones dated from the early 1800s.

We entered the church. Erin walked down the nave to the chancel where Shakespeare's body was entombed. She stood for a long time in front of a stained glass window with its depiction of Christ on the cross. Erin's stared at the flat tombstones embedded in the floor. On the left was Anne's tomb, with the inscription:

Here lyeth the wife of William Shakespeare who departed this life the 6th day of August 1623 being at the age of 67 yeares.

William Shakespeare's flat tombstone was scuffed and chipped. I was surprised at the small size of the letters of Shakespeare's "curse." Because the inscription on the stone was upside down to the viewer, a sign had been erected at the foot of the tomb:

> *Good Friend for Jesus SAKE forbeare*
> *To digg the Dust Enclosed HERe.*
> *Blessed be the Man yet spares these Stones*
> *And Curst, be He that moves my Bones*

Not very eloquent, I thought. I turned to the stone bust of Shakespeare, six feet above the tomb, showing the playwright with a feathered quill in one hand. I whispered to Erin, "I read that they give him a new quill once a year, one from an Avon River swan."

Erin didn't say anything, just concentrated on Shakespeare's tomb. Finally, she sighed, "I don't know." She took one last look at the stone tomb and turned away from the altar. Breathing deeply and expelling the air from her lungs in one long breath, she said, "I feel . . . nothing. There is *nothing* here."

I took her hand and rubbed it.

"I know you wanted me to find something, to see a ghost, but I can't just conjure up Shakespeare. It has to happen."

"Let's go," I said. *There is nothing to find,* I thought. *Just cold stone and tombs of dust.*

Leaving the church, we walked by the brown-and-white paneled school, in which Shakespeare was said to have learned

Latin and other studies. At the end of the block we heard chapel bells.

"Must be the old Guild Chapel," I said, checking my guidebook. "It's right across the street from where Shakespeare's retirement home once stood. The house was demolished hundreds of years ago. He and Anne probably walked across the street to come here to worship. Want to take a look inside the chapel?" I asked.

In a weary voice, she said, "Don't expect anything weird to happen."

We stepped into the chapel. It was one of the lesser-known stops on the tourist trail and no one was inside. A musty, unused smell permeated the place. The air seemed to hover lifelessly, as if waiting to be aroused by human visitors.

Erin slowly approached the small chancel. I lingered behind her, studying the fading wall murals that appeared to be done by an inept Middle Ages artist. I was about to mention this to Erin when I noticed her standing statue-like before the altar. Light coming through the stained glass windows created a multi-colored halo around her body.

There was not a sound.

I saw Erin's shudder and went to her side. She turned, eyes glazed. "I saw a woman crying . . . at the altar."

I stared at the altar, half expecting to see—what?

Erin sat down on one of the choir pews, visibly shaken. "There's an *energy* that flows through here." She focused on a single chair just under the archway that led to the chancel. "*There*, in that chair . . . *another* woman. No, it could be the same person." She stared blankly, irises like pinpoints. "I'm getting an image of a funeral procession. I see a casket draped in brocade, a cross over it. The woman is crying."

I stared at the chair, seeing nothing. "Does she have any form?"

"She's short, petite, with blonde curly hair."

"Do you think it's Anne?"

"I don't know," she said quietly and breathed deeply. "I don't know what she looked like. Are there any paintings of her?"

"The only thing I remember is a drawing, more like a quick sketch, that I saw in a book. The drawing shows an oval-faced woman in a cap with a fringe of what may be blonde hair, a ruff around her neck. Scholars say it might be of her."

Erin's eyes cleared, the spell broken. "The woman I saw could have been Anne," Erin said, still staring at the chair. "I still feel this strong— *energy*, something I didn't have at Holy Trinity Church or Anne's house. It's like a *divine* energy. I don't know how else to explain it. When I first stepped in here, I felt it go though my body. I can still *feel* it."

She saw Anne Shakespeare! I thought,

"I'm very tired." She dabbed at the perspiration on her forehead as I helped her up and walked out of the chapel with my arm around her waist.

I said. "Let go back to the hotel and rest, then have a nice dinner and a bottle of wine. Then—"

She looked at me with that wicked glint in her eyes. She seemed to be suddenly rejuvenated, her spirits high. She put her hand behind my neck, pulled my face to hers, and kissed me long and hard. I felt her body press into mine as she said, "I'm not really *that* tired."

"This may be cold," Erin said sometime later.

Eyes closed, I felt the cool drops of scented oil dribble down my back, pooling in the center of my spine as Erin squeezed the liquid from a bottle. One drop trickled on the terry-cloth bath towel she had spread on the bed.

"The oil, the smell. What is it?" I asked.

"Relax." She was straddling one of my legs. I could feel the bare skin of her thighs. I sniffed the air. "Jasmine?"

"It's an aphrodisiac. It's called Ylang Ylang." She spread the oil across my back with broad sweeping motions, then curved her hands around my shoulders, smoothing the oil into my skin. "It heats up the body."

I felt it, the strange warmth, and opened my eyes. In the flickering light from the candle, I could see the shadow of her nude body above me, her form artfully blurred as the light danced across her breasts. The candle was scented.

Lavender? I wondered.

Erin's palms pressed upward, thumbs digging into the cords of muscle on the ridge of my spine. Her fingers probed deep into my flesh.

"You're tight," she whispered. The point of her elbows replaced the fingers, pressing forcefully enough into muscle to crush my chest into the bed. I exhaled, and found I couldn't take a breath. Then the pressure relaxed, and I gratefully sucked in air.

Erin leaned forward and stretched her torso across my back. I could feel her breasts press into my skin, soaking up the oil. She rotated her chest, and the oil blended our bodies into one, creating a lubricated sheen between us.

Her fingers, thumbs, and elbows worked deeper into the skin and muscles of my back and shoulders, hands gliding across my hips, and then down my legs. My skin tingled from the heat generated by the oil, by the ceaseless maneuvering of her hands.

The motion stopped.

She sat up straight, waves of hair brushing erotically against my leg. She breathed two words, "Roll over."

I turned, and she straddled my legs again and I felt a light brush of hair.

The light from the candle created fleeting, abstract images on the wall. I saw the bottle of oil in her hand being squeezed. The fresh aroma of jasmine hit my nostrils, then I felt the splattering of drops on my chest. She began to massage, her fingers feathering through the tight curls of hair.

After a few minutes spreading and kneading the oil into the skin, Erin changed positions to the side of my body and ran her hands down, then up the inside of my thighs, slipping the flat of her palm between my legs.

I could feel her green eyes on me, hear her steady breathing, faster paced than it had been. She raised her hands higher and, in a circular motion, once more caressed my chest, then scooted away and leaned against a bundle of pillows.

"Anything else you want massaged?"

Later Erin would write the scene that followed, which I used in my novel, *To Be or Not To Be Shakespeare.* She said that since my character was female, the scene needed an erotic female viewpoint.

Silence. Then the sound of flickering candles infused the air like an erotic cloak. Her cheeks flushed at the heat of his fixed and decisive gaze. There was no response to her question, only an undercurrent of passion and the vulnerability of her naked body as he observed her. Then he took her hand into his and, for the first time ever, she felt safe in a man's arms.

She leaned forward and buried her face against the muscled chest, the sound of his heartbeat causing a teardrop of relief to fall and tangle itself in his chest hair. She quickly licked the salty remains away.

He wrapped her hair in his hands and pulled her toward him, kissing her slowly and tenderly, and then let her go as he buried his kisses into the hollow of her neck and explored the soft, feminine lines of her waist and hips. She could feel his uneven breathing and, in response, tucked her curves neatly into the contours of his body, letting his hands direct hers toward his sex.

Wisps of her hair fanned his skin as she trailed this gesture with her tongue, tracing an imaginary line from his chest to the tip. Palms still slick with oil, she took him into her hands and kneaded slowly, feeling his flesh harden. He waited, hardly breathing, for her to release him from her erotic touch. She stroked him, at times firm and demanding, and at other times, soft and gentle. Then, with a groan, he stopped her and turned over, grasping her hands into his and pressing them into the bed. His hands roamed over her breasts as he moved to touch her with his tongue.

She tensed and cried out in a whisper, "No." Instead, with her skin still prickling from the heat of his touch, she moved him across her body and guided him into her.

They moved in unison, savoring this moment of their intimacy as she murmured a quote from Shakespeare: "Two instruments lovingly played," then locked her legs around his waist. Her skin was alive with a sheen of moisture, her mouth next to his ear, breath quickening . . . and then she gave in to her body as it arched in ecstasy and in rhythm to his final movements.

After it was over, he supported his body on his elbows and knees, trying not to press his weight against hers. His muscles began to tremble, and she soothed his back, urging him to relax against her. They stayed like that for a long time, relishing the after-glow.

Later, still smelling of oil and sex, she smoothed the bed covers over his body, traced his lips with a fingernail, and then blew out the candle. A thin, sinuous ghost of smoke writhed upward.

Thank you, Erin

The next day Erin and I continued to tour Stratford-Upon-Avon, taking a carriage ride, doing a little shopping. I stopped at the Tourist Information Center, as I wanted to see if they had a book on Shakespeare that I had been trying to find. The lady behind the counter said it wasn't in stock, but she could order it and send it to me. I gave her my address.

Later at lunch, I noticed Erin staring at me with those fiery eyes. "You're going back to your wife."

This startled me. Although we both knew in our hearts what would happen, we'd never talked about it.

"I heard you give that tourist woman your wife's address."

"Yes." That was all I could say.

"When?"

"A week after we get back. When you fly to Washington to look for a house."

"You've told her this."

"Yes."

She rubbed her forehead and sighed. The fire faded from her eyes, and I saw softness, but no tears. "I'm not going to spoil the rest of our trip," she said in a voice I could barely hear. "I knew this was going to happen, so let's just let it be."

We never mentioned it again while we were in England, but the knowledge cast a shadow of sadness over the rest of the trip.

We returned to London without incident; my driving skills had improved after a week behind the wheel. Elizabeth was happy to see us back, unscathed, and applauded our safe return. She suggested we celebrate with a sumptuous dinner at one of her favorite restaurants.

"I have a better idea," I said. "I'd like to take Erin to a musical comedy."

"Great," Elizabeth said. "*The Lion King* is playing. It's fantastic."

"I want to get tickets to *Beauty and the Beast.*"

I felt Erin stiffen beside me. I turned to her, asking, "If that's all right with you?"

He eyes moistened. "Yes, I would like that."

Throughout the performance of *Beauty and the Beast* Erin sat quietly, never reacting to the performance, never smiling, never laughing, never crying. It was as if she'd shifted her mind to another plane of existence. Perhaps it had been cruel of me to bring her to the musical.

As we exited the theater, she stopped and kissed me lightly on the lips. "Thank you for bringing me," she said.

The next morning we prepared to leave for the airport. After getting dressed and having toast and coffee, I glanced at our itinerary, focusing on the time of our flight's departure: 9:30 AM! I looked at my watch: 9:35! Oh, shit!

I raced to Elizabeth. "We have a serious problem. I read the tickets wrong. Our flight has already departed."

She didn't say a word, just zipped into action and called the airport. After hanging up the phone, she said, "There's another flight we can make, but they only have few seats." She threw up both hands. "Let's go!"

We made a mad dash to the airport. As we skidded in front of the entry, Elizabeth jumped out and said, "Let me handle this."

We followed her, wheeling our luggage to a ticket reservation counter. To the man behind the counter, Elizabeth regally announced, "I am Lady Forthsyte, and these are my

American friends. We need to put them on the next flight to Los Angeles."

"Full," he said in typical English aplomb. "Except for Business Class."

I told him I'd upgrade on my Mileage Plus. He checked my total miles on his computer, noted I had over 20,000 for the upgrade, and issued a new ticket.

Then he checked Erin's mileage. She had less than 12,000 miles. "Sorry, I can't issue you a ticket."

Erin gave him a sensuous look with those jade-green eyes, smiled delightfully, and said, "Yes, you can."

"Why?" he asked, obviously startled.

"Because I'm cute."

We drank champagne all the way home.

Chapter 15

Happiness Is Where the Heart Is

E rin and I stood side by side on the balcony of our rented Santa Barbara condo listening to the birds squabbling in the trees. Neither of us looked at each other, nor did we speak. We had been back from England for two days and the reality of separating weighed heavily on our minds.

Erin looked haggard, dark shadows under her eyes, her cheeks pale. Finally she said, "We knew this day would come. You've made your decision and nothing I can do will change it."

"No."

"I guess one of the things I love about you, is you're the kind of man who'll always go back to his family." She turned to me, eyes wet. "But goddamn her! Goddamn your wife for loving you before I did."

Her words cut through me like a jagged knife. There was nothing I could say. My wife was expecting my return.

Erin had purchased an airline ticket to Seattle. She intended to rent a car, drive to the city of Port Townsend, and look for a house to buy, then return and get her furniture out of storage. She was far braver than I, willing to start a new life— alone. By the time she got back, I'd be gone from the condo. *Clean and neat,* I thought.

"You chose not to love me," Erin said, staring at a flicker of leaves in the trees.

"Please, Erin, let's not make this hard. Let's just part as friends." *God, that sounds so damn trite.*

"Why are we parting? I know you still love me, as I love you." She shook her head. "We have the chance to make each other happy for the rest of our lives. Now you're leaving me for another woman."

"The woman is my wife."

"I know that, goddamn it!" She was on fire again. Then, with a sigh, she rested her head on my shoulder; neither of us put our arms around each other. "Why did you let it go so far between us? A year! We've been together a year."

"We broke up nine months ago," I said.

"Oh, God, I was so wrong about that. I've tried to make it up to you. I've loved you—" She tightened her fists and pressed them hard to my chest as if she was readying to strike me. "Do you really love your wife?"

I wrapped my arms around her shaking body. "I don't have the courage to leave my wife and children to make a new life with you in some vague place I've never been. One part of me wants you more than anything else in the world, the other part tells me I must return to my family."

She raised her head. "And if doesn't work out between you and your wife?"

"Then you'll see me barking like a dog in front of your new home. I know one thing: You've changed my life. You made me feel young again, made me feel loved."

She breathed in deeply. "So this is how it ends."

"Yes."

Suddenly, she brightened. "Then let's make the last days perfect." She kissed me deeply, and I tasted her rising passion.

For the next two days, we did little else but make love, rest, talk, and then make love again.

I drove her to the airport. When her flight was called, I kissed her goodbye and watched as she walked across the concrete to the boarding ladder. At the top, she turned, and, as she always did, my love, my dearest love, waved tiny fingers at me.

Then, she was gone.

At the condo, tears streaming down my face, I wrote a farewell note.

> *Erin,*
>
> *As I drove away from the airport, the car radio was playing an old Doris Day song, "I'll Never stop Loving You," and I wondered, How did Erin manage to do that? I guess because you're cute.*
>
> *Cute.*
>
> *I remember one morning . . . you were kneeling on the floor surrounded by a pile of shoes, green eyes wide, and I joked, "How could anyone love a red-haired ragamuffin?" You cocked your head. "Because I'm cute."*
>
> *Cute. No, more than that: Beautiful. Adorable. Loving. Sexy.*
>
> *On our trip back from New Orleans and the Delta Queen, we were waiting for our flight departure, and I went to get a cup of coffee. When I returned you were reading, legs crossed in a short skirt, and I stopped and stared at you for a long time, thinking – I really love this girl. And at that moment, I did love you more than life itself. As I have done on so many other occasions.*
>
> *We will both remember . . . Beauty . . . Beast . . . that first kiss . . . sunsets . . . Catalina . . . the Delta Queen: New Year's Eve; you in that shimmering red dress. Christmas Eve at the Mission when our love*

wedded . . . A Glastonbury sunrise and that mystic pearl
disc on The Tor. Stratford-Upon-Avon . . . sharing our
writing . . . telling each other how brilliant the other was
(and meaning it) . . . the lovemaking . . . the love. . . the
eternal love . . .

    No, it was a lot more than cute.

    Now, when I think of you and brush the tears
from my eyes, I will be filled with joy.

    For I have loved.

    And been loved—

    Clay

I brought my wife a bouquet of flowers.

Chapter 16

Home Again

It was good to be in familiar surroundings, the furniture, paintings on the walls. The smell of my wife's cooking. Strangely, I didn't feel like her husband.

But I did something for my wife—I helped to restore her health. A month earlier I had visited her at the polo condo to tell her I would return to her after the England trip. (She later admitted that she almost told me not to bother to come home if I went on another trip with "that person.") I found her on the couch that day, holding her stomach, in deep pain. When I asked what was the matter, she answered, "Stress, the doctor says, because of our situation."

"I'm coming back, it will only be a month. Is the doctor sure about stress?"

"He's giving me tranquilizers. Sometimes the pain goes away."

At the time I wondered if she was pretending, a method to insure I returned. Her illness was one of the factors that heightened my return, although I never told Erin this. Yet, when I walked in with the flowers, my wife was resting on the sofa, still in pain.

"This is more than stress," I said, kneeling beside her and offering the flowers. "There's something wrong."

The next day the pain intensified, so I took her to her doctor, who finally diagnosed kidney stones. It was a quick operation to rid her kidneys of the stones. Shortly thereafter she was back to normal.

I wasn't.

She was more demanding than ever. *As she should be*, I thought. I was required to have blood tests to insure I was squeaky clean. She also set up several sessions for us with a marriage counselor. We went together to the first session. The female counselor, a brittle young woman, asked questions with a knowing smile on her lips. I didn't like her anymore than I did the livid yellow walls of her office.

"Why did you leave your wife and family for this other woman?" she asked.

I wanted to say, "Because I love her." But my wife was there so I answered, "Old-age crisis." I wanted to add, "Erin is young, attractive, exiting, and sexier than hell," but I bit my tongue and said nothing more.

"Are you still *seeing* her?"

"No, she moved to Washington State."

"I asked if you are still *seeing* her."

The questions went on and on, probing, constantly probing. I felt like I was undergoing a police interrogation.

The next session, I went alone. My wife had already had her "single" session. The counselor started by saying, "I can see you've had the best of both worlds, a loving wife, and a young woman to toy with."

I stood up. "I really don't like your yellow walls," I said, and left.

After that, I was thrust back into the social whirl of parties, charity events and theater. Although a few friends said, "I'm so happy you're back," most of them looked at me with embarrassed expressions on their faces. Others shunned me completely. I was the adulterer, the fool who'd left a perfect marriage for, what they thought of as, that "redheaded bimbo."

Once in a while some guy would smirk at me and ask, "How was the babe in bed?"

I couldn't lash back at them, so I just ignored the comments.

At a party I would slip away from the incessant din of cocktail chatter and stare at the moon, watch the ocean, just find a quiet spot and talk to Erin. I felt she could hear me. At one party, I asked a pianist if he could play, "Somewhere in Time." When I heard the familiar notes, I immersed myself in memories of Erin.

My wife remained ever vigilant. As it turned out, she was right to suspect me of maintaining my ties to Erin.

I don't think I would have contacted Erin, and was surprised when I received an e-mail from her. She said she'd bought a house in Port Townsend and would be back in Santa Barbara to have her furniture shipped from storage. She asked if I would see her for lunch.

I stared at the letter for a long time. We'd separated, said goodbye one last time. I was never supposed to see her again. I had promised.

Erin and I met at a restaurant on the opposite side of town. I was terrified that someone would spot us. Erin told me about her new home, which she adored, and that she had found a cat she named Merlin. "It's nice to have a heartbeat around my home."

I said very little, only that I was getting along, and that it was tougher to go back than I'd expected. What I wanted to say was, "Erin, let's get out of town and watch sunsets together for the rest of our lives."

When she drove off in Beauty, her black BMW, she stuck one hand out the window and waved with tiny, loving fingers.

Two weeks later my wife confronted me with my Master Card statement. She pointed to an item. "Why were you at this restaurant?"

I looked at the entry. I hadn't realized I'd used my credit card to pay for the lunch. Stumbling for words, I lied. "Her son, he called, said he wanted to see me."

She crumpled the paper and threw the statement at me. "You are never to see him again."

I knew my every move would be watched even more closely. I had left a loving relationship with Erin for one in which I was no longer master of my house, nor master of my own life. I couldn't blame my wife. I would have had the same reaction if she'd left me for another man, then returned.

I went for a long walks on the polo fields. When I was far enough away that no one but the sky could hear, I yelled in frustration, "Erin! I love you!"

Chapter 17

Chaos

*G*oddamn you to hell!* The first words of Erin's e-mail startled me, as did the rest of the letter.

I'm sitting at my computer, crying and surrounded by boxes that haven't been unpacked. I'm sick, not just physically, but mentally. My asthma is tearing me apart. I can hardly breathe. Walking from my bedroom to the kitchen is a nightmare.

The move to Port Townsend was a disaster. The guys who took my stuff from storage and jammed it into the van were total assholes. They banged up my beautiful baby grand piano, scratched my mother's antique chairs, and left me watching them, sitting on a cold stone step, bawling my eyes out.

I am alone because of you. You left me, when all I wanted was to be loved and cared for by the man I love.

Fuck you.

I reread the letter several times, the darkening shadow of her weariness, of sadness, of her emotional rage enveloping my mind and body. My heart ached for her. At this moment she reminded me of a little girl lost in the woods.

The next day, I received another e-mail.

Dearest Clay,
I just reread my e-mail from yesterday. Glad I got that off my
chest—bosom, whatever. No, I wasn't that angry woman you
have seen. No, it wasn't a mood swing. It was just me, sad and
bitchy. I woke up fresh this morning and decided to get on with
my life.
I called a doctor in Port Townsend and have set up an
appointment tomorrow. I need help. I desperately need help to
deal with my emotions.
I will live my life without you. I'll never forget you and
will always cherish the wonderful moments we've had. If you
feel like it, write to me, at least as a friend.
Love, Erin

So, we began our e-mail correspondence again. I knew I
was betraying my wife and hated myself for it. But Erin was
like a taste of honey and I couldn't resist the allure of her scent.

I escorted my wife to social events and joked that I was
her consort. From outward appearances, we were once again the
perfect couple, but something essential had changed within the
structure of our marriage. When we weren't around others, I
showed little affection. I didn't take her hand when we went on
walks. At times, she would put her arm through mine, as she
used to do, and it felt good. But when she did, I didn't think of
her and how happy I should be—I thought of Erin. I regretted
my stiffness at those times, and I knew I was treating her
miserably. It had to be obvious to her that I wasn't the same
husband she had once known. Yet, I couldn't alter my own
reality. My heart and my thoughts were in Washington State.

This was proven to me two months after Erin left when I received an e-mail in which she wrote, rather off-hand, *I'm dating a doctor.*

I couldn't believe how that simple phrase tore at me. My girl dating! Yet, I had no hold over her. I told her in the next e-mail that I knew she would be dating and, perhaps, find someone with whom to share her life. *Please don't tell me about it*, I wrote. She answered:

Don't worry, Mr. Jealous. I'm not going out with him again. There is no interest there. Port Townsend has a bunch of weird men, none of them my kind.

Although I was relived, I knew she would find someone. She was young, a new girl in town, and terribly attractive.

She told me she was working again on her Goddess novel, which she hadn't done since our trip to England. Her method of writing was far different from mine: She called on the "Otherworld." In an e-mail, she told me how it worked:

Good morning! Had a good night's sleep last night – a good one, very productive. I dreamed again about my Goddess book. I love it when that happens. Not every night, but most nights. The dreams take me back to my ancestral memories and show me what to write – show me the terrain and the people in the Otherworld realm. From what I have researched, this is a common occurrence in Irish Celtic people like myself. Sometimes it's uncanny, as it doesn't seem possible for me to "know" these things – then, when I research, I find documented fact to substantiate my knowledge.
Strange, huh?
Not really, because this happens to me all of the time.

I wrote back, saying that I understood and no longer reservations about believing her psychic abilities. I also said I loved her. I didn't use the word as a friend. Her reply, when it arrived, revealed a calmer Erin.

Your heart reached out beyond time and space and touched me. I miss being in you arms. And yes, you have come a long way in trying to understand me – but all I ever really wanted was your acceptance and the freedom to express myself without fear of your rejection. Your effort in really trying to understand and communicate, I have to admit, makes my heart sing. No one has ever cared enough to find out how I tick, let alone understand the depth of my feelings and knowledge. And yes, there is a lot more. Hold on—
I awakened at 3AM this morning and spent time reading. Found a chapter on the Holy Grail that described something interesting that I believe had something to do with the stigmata on my clothing—

I stopped reading at this point, remembering what she had told me shortly after she moved to Washington, something that had disturbed me. She said she had awakened in the night and found spots of blood on her nightclothes, blood that had not come from her body as there were no cuts or wounds. I'd had a difficult time with that, but I had learned to believe. With Erin anything was possible. I went back to reading the letter:

Well, anyway, I had an epiphany – yet still can't put it into words. All I can say is that I received a special blessing – and I KNOW the goddess book must be written. I also believe that this is the reason I have been placed in isolation. I am beginning to get more information and, well, the silence helps my inner healing.

*See? I already shared something. And speaking
of sharing, it will seem strange this New Year's Eve not to
celebrate 2000 with you. But when midnight comes, I will toast
a glass of champagne to you and send you my love. You will
have one consolation – I will be with my sister on her couch
and not yukking it up with another man. You, however, will
have someone in your arms. Something that has been very
difficult for me to adjust to these last few months when I think of
you – especially at night. I try to erase that from my mind,
because it tears me up too much.*

At the New Year's charity party I attended with my
wife, I found time to get slip away from the crowd, look at the
stars, lift a glass of champagne, and whisper, "I love you, Erin."

To keep my mind off the things that were wrong in my
life, I accelerated my work on *To Be or Not To Be Shakespeare.*
I sent Erin the last chapter to read. She praised it, once again
calling my writing "brilliant."

On impulse, I wrote: *I'm going to dedicate Shakespeare
to you.*

She answered: *That's a nice gesture and I love you for
it, but I know that can never be.*

I wrote back, *Yes, it can, I promise.*

From that moment on, five months after Erin and I had
parted, I knew I was living a lie with my wife.

The e-mails that Erin and I exchanged grew more
affectionate in tone. It was as if we'd started all over again as
Beauty and the Beast, back to the days during which our first
letters had led us into a romance. Of course, I felt pangs of
excruciating guilt as I came to a new realization.

I was going to leave my wife.

For the second time.

Two months later Erin flew to Santa Barbara to see her son. We made arrangements to meet. I drove her to a secluded park and opened a bottle of red wine.

"You're beautiful," I said, staring at her profile. She was wearing a white warm-up suit and tennis shoes.

She plucked at the jacket. "I look like a bleached teddy bear. Hardly sexy."

Neither of us said anything for a while, just enjoyed the wine and the nearness of each other. Finally, she said, "We never should have split up. I don't mean six months ago—that was your idea—but the first time—"

"When you told me to leave."

"Someone else did that," she said, tilting the glass to her lips. "I should have talked it out with you. That's something we never did, talk about our differences. We just went on, hoping the gods would take care of us."

They didn't, I thought

"I feel I'm healthier now, more in control of my emotions."

"It can't be easy living alone," I said.

"I have my cat, Merlin."

"Do you think we'd have a chance, if we got together again?" I asked, then said, "I have to be sure."

She waited a moment before answering, swirling the wine in her glass as if looking for an answer in the pool of dark liquid. Then: "We've learned a lot about each other these last months."

"The hard way." I knew I was pressing her, but I needed answers.

She took my hand in hers. "I don't feel we can live without each other."

I touched her cheek. She turned to me and we kissed, spilling a little wine on her white jacket. "I hope that's a good omen," I said. But deep inside I felt it might be a bad one.

It looked like blood.

Erin returned to Washington and I began, once again, to search my mind for a way to tell my wife I was leaving her. It would be harder this time, so much harder. This time, strong woman or not, it might destroy her.

I told Erin I would inform her when to fly back to Santa Barbara so I could accompany her back to Washington. I would have to pack up, rent a U-haul truck and a carrier to tow my car. I set the Fourth of July as the date I would leave Santa Barbara. Erin agreed. Then something happened. That "person" came back into our lives.

Erin sent me an e-mail in which she stated she had consulted her astrology charts (something she never did in my presence) and decided she would have to sell her stocks because of what she saw in the stars. "Black Monday," she called it. I should have trashed the letter and forgot about it, but it disturbed me enough to write back:

Some time ago I asked if you would show me, or demonstrate your belief in astrology so I could learn and understand. You demurred, saying (as I recall) you were not interested anymore. I dropped the subject and it never came up again. That is, until you mentioned your fear of a "Black Monday" and the decline of the stock market, and that you were considering selling stocks predicated on the alignment of the planets and stars. I am trying hard, but I guess I just don't know how strong your astrological beliefs are.

I know this is ludicrous to say, but does this mean our

marriage will be based on the action of the planets and stars?
Will our marriage succeed or dissolve because of what you read
in the alignment of some planets? Or do you, like I, believe in
the faith of a God-given union between two people who love
each other so much?

In my life as a navy pilot, I flew far too many times into
the dark abyss of the unknown, placing my life on the line, but
always knowing I would survive because of my skills. My
training. My knowledge. My understanding of the fierce
elements I was encountering.

Without your help, I feel like I am once again entering
the unknown. This time with no skills, no knowledge, no
understanding.

Please lead me.

Don't send this letter! I screamed at myself, finger
hovering over the "Send" icon. *Believe in her.* What she said is
meaningless, I told myself.

Then I clicked, "Send."

The letter I received in return wasn't just angry. It was
that of a woman *enraged.* A woman I didn't know.

It was the other Erin.

The letter was almost incoherent, a jumble of words as if
they spewed from a serpent's mouth: *Bastard, you don't believe*
anything I believe in! I have a life you will never understand.
Fuck you, again and again . . . fuck you . . .

I stopped reading in dismay and deleted the letter, then
sat for a long time, coming to the realization I could never live
with this "other" person that Erin could become. Her mood
swings contained venom that staggered me. I decided I couldn't
answer the letter.

The next morning I got a phone call from Erin, something we had agreed she would never do. I had no idea when my wife would be at home.

In a voice no more than a flutter, Erin said, "Clay?"

"Erin, you can't—"

"No, don't hang up. Please . . ."

I didn't answer, just stared at the phone in my hand.

From what sounded like a far distance, I heard, "Please, listen to me. I know I did a terrible thing. So terrible, I—"

I heard her crying and my shoulders sagged. Then, in a birdlike voice, she continued. "I had another of my mood swings. I reread the letter and cried all night. I was afraid you wouldn't read my e-mails, so I had to call."

"Erin, I—"

"Just try and listen, please. I called my doctor and told him about my problem. He believes I have a chemical imbalance and said there was a hormone I could take that would soften my anger so it will never happen again."

"Erin, I don't think any pill—"

Her voice trembled. "Can we just try?"

I didn't know what to think, except feel sorry for her. She had finally recognized she had a problem and was going to do something about it. But could I take a chance on a doctor's prescription for something I felt was greater than what a simple pill could remedy? I sighed and told Erin I'd have to think about it. "Write to me and tell me what effect you think the hormone is having on you," I said as I hung up.

As I said this, I heard a voice in my ear, asking, *What's it like too feel so passionate about someone, you are willing to sacrifice everything?* I didn't have the answer.

The next day I went with my wife to see a movie. One of the previews was about a woman who braved the elements of

Africa. The hype announced, "She dared to leave everything she knew and loved."

She dared. Did I?

Then I read a quote in the newspaper, "In life we have 1000 chances, all we have to do is take one."

A day later, as I clicked through television channels, I happened to stop on a sitcom in which the male character said to another man, "I gotta marry this girl. I don't want to find myself in old age sitting in a wheelchair sucking yellow Jell-O through a straw, knowing I'd never taken a chance."

It was at that moment I knew I was going to take the chance. No matter how many different temperaments there were to her personality, I deeply loved this strange Irish redhead with the jade-green eyes.

A week later I told my wife I couldn't live a lie anymore.

It just happened. We had gone to a restaurant for breakfast, and, as I was fumbling in my billfold for money to pay the bill, I happened to pull out a folded slip of paper that had addresses on it, including Erin's Washington address. When we got home, I sat on the terrace with a cup of coffee and my wife came out a moment later with the slip of paper. She had taken it out of my billfold. When she confronted me with the address, I said, "I can't live without her."

We talked calmly for a while. The only thing I remember her saying was:

"God, I hate this."

And my weak reply: "I am so sorry, so terribly sorry."

I had betrayed her. Again.

Chapter 18

An Enchanted Cottage

With a ribbon, I tied the diamond engagement ring on the stem of the white rose. Erin was not expecting this.

She had arrived at the airport in Santa Barbara that afternoon, stepping through the plane's hatch, squinting in the bright sunlight. She looked in the direction of the waiting crowd who were meeting friends and relatives. Although she couldn't see me in the milling people, she waved her fingers as she always did, then hurried across the concrete apron in her high heels and a moment later she was in my arms.

We held each other for a long time.

I had made reservations at a beachside hotel. I brought a bottle of champagne and fluted glasses. After we checked into the room, I said, "Let's have a glass of champagne by the beach and watch the sunset." I handed her the white rose.

She hugged me tightly and said, "I'll always love you." She didn't see the diamond and started to put the rose in a glass of water, but I said, "Better bring it with you."

We walked to the grass by the edge of the breaking waves and toasted with the champagne. She sniffed the rose, her lip inches from the diamond. The late afternoon sun caught glints from the stone's many facets and sparkled in her eyes.

"Oh, my God," she said, seeing the ring. And the tears came, tears of joy.

We embraced and knew it was right. We'd finally found our perfect place in time.

The next day we slid onto the worn bench seats of the U-Haul truck, and with my car, "The Prince"—as Erin called it—chained to a four-wheel carrier behind the truck, we drove onto the freeway and headed north to Washington. To a home I had never seen.

The three-day trip was like a joy ride to a couple of teenagers who were going on their first date, chattering incessantly, hour after hour, learning things they had never known about each other, never had time to ask, never took the time to talk about. The truck laboriously chugged its way across the flatland of southern California with its vineyards, then through the frenzied freeways of San Francisco, climbing past snow-capped Mt. Shasta, continuing north to Oregon with its evergreen trees, then churned through the smog of Portland and up the curving road to the Olympic Peninsula.

Then, home.

When I stepped into Erin's house, I was captivated. The cathedral ceiling created a sanctuary of space and made the living room bright and airy. Picture windows opened to a forest of leaves, the evergreen trees so close I felt I could touch the rough bark. The kitchen was open to a dining area where Erin had placed her baby grand piano. There was a fireplace, fronted by overstuffed couches.

"Erin, I love it!" I grabbed her by the waist and twirled her around.

"It's ours," Erin said proudly. "It's our home, our—"

"Enchanted cottage," I finished.

We settled in quickly, unloading the boxes from the U-Haul and rolling the Prince off the carrier. I drove him into the garage and reintroduced him to Erin's BMW, Beauty.

"Think they'll do anything while we're not watching?" Erin asked, her arm around my waist.

"Won't we?"

"I guess they deserve to be together again."

I pulled Erin away. "We'd better close the garage door. I think the Prince's hood is heating up."

"Um, hum, and Beauty's beginning to breathe heavily."

That's the way we were, silly, giddy, and so happy. Nothing could ever change that.

Nothing.

I put my computer and desk into a bedroom and placed it in front of the mullioned windows so I could see and hear the trees rustling in the breeze, watch deer saunter through the front yard, and chuckle at a family of raccoon as they waddled past. Multi-hued birds fluttered and squabbled in the trees.

We were living in a gated housing area, and I soon discovered it was more like a retirement community. Although there were a few young couples with school age children, I guessed the median age of the homeowners to be in their mid-seventies.

"I'll bet the number one activity around here is aluminum walker races," I told Erin.

We went to a New Resident's Mixer at the clubhouse to meet some of the homeowners. We never heard so many people say, "It's nice to have young people around. We're old."

As we left, Erin said, "I vow never to say, 'I'm old.' "

Hugging her, I answered, "Coco Chanel, the fashion designer, once said something like, 'Someday I'll be sixty, then seventy, and eighty, but I'll never be old.' "

Erin's body pressed against mine. "I'll keep you young."

Erin took me on a tour of Port Townsend, with its Victorian houses, quaint shops, and curving beach that overlooked Puget Sound and snowcapped Mt. Hood. A lighthouse completed the fantasy picture. I fell in love with Port Townsend.

But it wasn't Santa Barbara.

Erin and I decided that we could live in both places— July through December in Port Townsend, the other six months in Santa Barbara where would rent an apartment near the beach. All we had to move was our clothes, computers, a few writing files and her cat, Merlin. This was too much to haul in Erin's BMW, or my sport car, so we bought a Subaru Outback SUV.

We also bought us another treat, a 7-day cruise to Alaska. Erin had never been on a cruise except for the Delta Queen Steamboat. Because of Erin's asthma, we booked a stateroom with a balcony. We told the maitre 'd that we were on our honeymoon (which we felt as if we were) and requested a table for two. We dined on fine cuisine, drank fine wine, danced, then retired to our room to hold each other throughout the night. Erin, always adventurous and innovative, suggested we make love on the frigid balcony of our stateroom.

"I'll freeze my—"

She snuggled up to me. "I'll keep you warm."

That night, we put on white terrycloth robes, sweat socks, and ventured outside where the temperature was near freezing. It was a clear night, the whispering sound of the ship cutting through the water a pleasant reminder that we were sailing through Alaskan waters. I smelled the pristine salt air, looked up at the smiling quarter-moon, and thought: *It's colder than hell out here.*

Under Erin's direction, I reclined on the plastic lounge chair; she opened my robe, and hers, and with the Alaskan night enveloping us, we made love.

I damn near froze my balls off.

Erin was deep into writing *The Goddess Spot,* and I was sending query letters to agents looking for representation to sell *To Be or Not To Be Shakespeare.* I received a letter back from a New York who requested the complete manuscript. For a month I hardly breathed. Then the letter came, which said in part:

> *Dear Clay Mills,*
> *I strongly feel I can sell To Be or Not To Be Shakespeare. It's a fun romp.*

I made revisions as directed by the agent, and *Shakespeare* was sent to an impressive list of major publishers. Then the rejections started arriving: "It's a rollicking ride," one said. "A fun book," a second one wrote. Another offered this praise: "An entertaining and quirky search for the real Shakespeare." Then this one: "Fascinating and controversial." All of the publishing houses liked *Shakespeare,* yet not one would take a chance on it. I went through a "wrist-slashing" period, as I tried to shake off my disappointment.

It was Erin who got my mind off the book

One evening, after we had settled down in front of the fireplace—It was now November and the weather had chilled—Erin said, "As you know, we've been engaged almost four months."

"Umm, hmm," I hummed, savoring a taste of Washington State Pinot Noir.

She scooted toward me on the couch. "Let's get married."

Married!

"Hey, don't look so surprised. That's what engaged couples do, marry."

"Well, yes, I know, but—"

"I've been good, haven't I?"

We both knew what she was talking about—her mood swings. We hadn't had one shred of an argument since we'd become engaged.

"You know," I said clicking the rim of my wineglass to hers, my face serious, "I've had enough of this living in sin stuff. We should get married!"

"Oh, honey, I thought you'd never ask!" She kissed me. "I love you"—kiss—"I love you!"—kiss—"I dearly love you!"

"When?" I asked, untangling myself from her spider web of arms.

"I have it all planned. I've been collecting different layers of clothing for my wedding dress. It will be old-fashioned, a little Victorian. I found my wedding hat, it's gorgeous, you'll love it." Her excitement escalated. "I want to be married in December. We can leave here by then, get a place on the beach. We'll be married—"

"Where?" I was able to slip this word in.

"I told you, remember?"

I did. The first time we went to Catalina and stayed at the Inn on Mt. Ada, she said, *I'm going to be married here someday*. "Catalina," I said.

"It's perfect!" She was practically jumping from her seat with excitement. "We'll get married overlooking Avalon, just the two of us. You'll wear your tux, I'll get someone to perform the wedding service, and we'll need a photographer." She paused and her eyes saddened. "I don't feel I can ask my son."

I knew this hurt her deeply. She did it because I couldn't invite my children. They were incensed that I had left their mother for the second time, as well they should be.

"Oh, honey," Erin said, breaking me away from my dreary thoughts, "We'll be even more in love after we're married."

I downed a mouth full of wine and gulped.

Married!

Chapter 19

Love and Marriage

*H**ow did I get here?* I wondered. It had been forty years since my first marriage. I couldn't possibly be doing this again. But here I was sitting in Ada Wrigley's small lounge that led to the bedroom, watching Erin primp before an antique dressing table mirror. To calm myself, I was reading an old book that I had found on the Inn in Mt. Ada's bookshelf.

We had arrived in Santa Barbara two weeks earlier. Unfortunately, the apartment complex by the beach that we wanted to stay in wouldn't have a vacancy for another month. We decided we could wait that out and get another place. The only beach apartment available as a weekly rental was a disaster. When we walked in, everything was covered in dust, the living area furniture spewed stuffing, the bed sagged like an Indian bow and the bathroom smelled of mold and urine. I had the manager clean the place—he pulled out a plywood board to stiffen the bed—before we took occupancy. The apartment did have a balcony with sunburned plastic chairs and a view of the beach. At least we could go to sleep in the sagging bed listening to the sounds of waves.

Erin and I dubbed it, Slum Shores.

"Look at it this way," I told her, "we're going to be in Catalina for three days, then ten days over New Year's cruising the Tahitian Island Islands on our honeymoon. We'll only have to live in this grubby ghetto for two weeks. Think of it as an enchanted cottage with a wicked witch."

Erin looked askance at the dusty floor. "She needs a better broomstick."

It was a relief to arrive in Catalina. Erin's carried two dozen white roses. She'd made arrangements for a minister to conduct the service, and hired a photographer. The only thing I was allowed to do was bring a bottle of champagne, pack my tux—and make sure I attended the wedding.

Erin was lovely as she sat in front of an antique mirror in Ada's Wrigley's sitting room, carefully putting on makeup before the wedding. I would glance up from the book I was reading and watch her in wonder.

Erin's wedding dress was a chiffon delicacy, layers and layers of cream and white tulle that flowed in waves to her ankles. She wore a wide-brimmed hat that was as light and airy as delicate frosting.

We stood on the terrace as the lady minister conducted the service. The weather had blessed us this December 18, 2000 with clear skies and a pleasant 70 degrees. I slipped the wedding ring on Erin's finger, saying, "I do," then watched the glow on her cheeks and the luster in her eyes as she said, "I do."

We didn't want to leave the Inn on Mt. Ada. It was our sanctuary, our citadel of love. We promised each other we would return each year on our anniversary.

Forever.

Back at Slum Shores, we bought a small fake Christmas tree—our Charlie Brown tree—and celebrated Christmas Day on the balcony, listening to the breaking waves. The temperature was in the mid-seventies, the sky clear as we opened packages. A few days later we flew to Tahiti to board a Renaissance cruise ship.

This time we didn't have to fib to the maitre 'd about being honeymooners.

At each Tahitian Island in which the ship anchored, I rented a car and we toured the island, searching for a private beach. Erin loved my adventuresome spirit, and we spent many hours in the warm, clear waters. But the treat Erin loved best was swimming with dolphins, a special activity offered by one of the resort hotels.

I bought diving masks and flippers on the ship. Since Erin had never snorkeled before, I showed her how to use the equipment in the ship's pool. "In the ocean, it'll be more fun," I said. "You'll see lots of fish."

"Fish!" Her eyes widened. "I can't swim with fish. They'll nibble at my toes."

"You're going to be in the water with dolphins."

She smirked. "Yes, but they're mammals."

In the dolphin pool, under the watchful guide of the dolphin attendant, we put on our diving masks and slipped into the water. Erin put her face below the blue surface and came up sputtering. "Fish! It's full of fish."

I looked down and saw hundreds of multi-hued fish, doing a ballet, darting in the underwater rays of the sun. I urged Erin to look again and this time she came up smiling. "It's another world."

We were introduced to two dolphins, a male and female, and were allowed to stroke their slick skin, swim along with them, throwing hoops for them to chase, and dive with them. The attendant said, "Be careful where you stroke the male dolphin. He has a tendency to get hard."

Erin's smiled wickedly.

The last evening, we took a cruise on a catamaran, enjoying the sunset and a full-moon rising magically over the pinnacle of Bora Bora.

"Our life is one made in heaven," Erin said as the horizon turned scarlet. She pressed her head to my shoulder. "I pray it never ends."

We managed to survive the last week at Slum Shores, then moved into our spacious, furnished, two-story apartment. The apartment had recently been refurbished and was spotless. We set up our computer laptops in two separate bedrooms, saving the master bedroom with its view of the mountains for ourselves.

The final two letters of rejection for *To Be or Not To Be Shakespeare* arrived and I asked myself, what do I do now?

That's when Erin discovered Time Warner iPublish.

"Look at this," she said, holding a sheaf of papers she'd printed out from her computer. "It's a new on-line program that Time Warner has established. Says it's devoted to discovering new talent. Why not submit *Shakespeare* and see what happens?"

"*Polo Wives*, too!" This was an erotic novel I had completed in a fury of writing when Erin and I had separated.

A few months after submission of the novels, both were put on the "Editor Favorites" list for several weeks, but I didn't receive any calls from the editors.

"So what do we do?" Erin asked.

There was only one answer: "Wait."

I received a travel invitation from European Waterways, a company who booked weeklong trips on luxury river barges throughout France, German, Ireland and Scotland. They wanted me to go on the Shannon Princess in Ireland. I wrote back, saying, "Can we match this trip with the barge, Scottish Highlander?" I advised that I had two magazines, which would accept the stories I wrote. They responded positively.

That evening, I asked Erin, "Of all the places in the world, where would you like to travel the most?"

She answered immediately. "Ireland. I've always wanted to go. Remember, I told you that my mother was born in North Ireland in Down Patrick near Belfast." Then she looked at me closely, suspecting something. "Why?"

"Why don't you pack your bags?"

"You're kidding." She jumped up. "No, you're *not* kidding."

"Nope, my wee, red-headed Irish lassie." I tried not to grin.

"Maybe we could find the *picture*," she said, almost to herself, "the one I know is in Ireland. The picture of *us* somewhere in time."

I didn't say anything, allowing myself to simply enjoy her joy. Although I believed in her clairvoyant abilities, a picture of *us* from the past was still beyond me. Finally, I said, "While we're over there, why don't we also take an excursion to Scotland and look for Nessie, the Lock Ness monster."

Ah, Erin loved me that night.

We flew into London and then on to Ireland, then rented a car and drove to Dingle Peninsula on the southwest shore of Ireland. Since we were going to drive on to Dublin where we would board the luxury barge, I asked the Hertz agent how much farther it was to Belfast in Northern Ireland.

"Sorry, sor," he said in a thick brogue, "But we canna allow our cars to go into the north. 'Tis the 'troubles,' you know."

Erin was saddened by this, but said, "No matter, we'll find my mother's home another time."

The luxury barges were a new way of cruising for both of us. You had to get lucky with your co-passengers, of which there were ten. But the cuisine and wines were exceptional, the conversation stimulating.

On the third day of the trip I noticed Erin talking to the young captain of the barge, and his pretty wife, who worked as the chef. I overheard Erin say, "Did you have a dog?"

The woman's eyes moistened. "She died two weeks ago, we miss her terribly."

As the young couple listened, astonished at her words, Erin described the dog, adding. "I saw her this morning on top of the pilot house."

"Why, that's where she always stood," the woman said, staring at Erin in awe.

Erin touched the woman's arm. "Your dog will always be with you, this is her home, she loves you too much to leave."

As I love you, my dearest Erin, I thought, knowing that my clairvoyant lady had brought comfort and peace to the young couple.

The barge trip was relaxing. We ate and drank too much, as we did when we boarded the Scottish Highlander a week later with a new hodge-podge of passengers.

We never saw Nessie.

When we returned to Santa Barbara, we were disappointed that there weren't any messages from a Time Warner editor.

"We wait," I told Erin again.

It was late June and time for the Santa Barbara Writers Conference. On the second day I got a call on my cell phone.

"Hello, I'm the romance editor of the Time Warner iPublish. I just read you novel, Polo Wives, and all I can say is, 'Wow!' "

Wow!

She went on to say that Time Warner wanted to publish *Polo Wives* for a December release and added that she'd e-mail a contract, and did I have any questions.

Wow!

Erin made her own pathway to recognition as a novelist. She had read excerpts of *The Goddess Spot* in both the conference's Women's Fiction workshop and the Fantasy workshop. At the end of the week, when the writing awards were passed out, she won First Place in Fantasy writing—and First Place in Women's Fiction.

Wow!

We were both ecstatic. Our work as writers, working together, helping each other in our first full year together was paying off. We drove back to Washington to hibernate and write, our heads in the clouds.

We had no idea that there was a dark, foreboding cloud hanging over our dreams.

Chapter 20

Tomorrow is Forever

It began the second week in November. We'd been back in our Port Townsend home for a little over four months, enjoying our idyllic retreat, taking long walks each day on the forest trails, enjoying the wildlife.

Erin was progressing well on her novel. I had completed the rewrites on *Polo Wives* for Time Warner iPublish. The novel was scheduled for publication January 1, a great way to start the New Year: We'd even booked a seven-day Caribbean cruise to celebrate.

Life was good. Life was great. Erin liked to say, "Tomorrow is forever."

Then came that day in November.

We'd just begun our walk, when Erin suddenly stopped. She was breathing laboriously. "I can't go on," she said. "Guess my asthma is acting up." She coughed, a deep racking sound that alarmed me. I took her back to the house, heated a cup of green tea, and urged her lie down on the sofa. "I'll be okay," she said as a deer sauntered up to the window above her and pressed its nose against the glass. Erin waved a few fingers and the deer sprinted away. "I'll be okay," she repeated.

But she wasn't.

Erin couldn't take walks during the following week. I grew increasingly more concerned. "You had a complete physical, what, two months ago?"

"August first," Erin confirmed. "The doctor said everything was okay."

"How'd your chest X-ray turn out?"

"He didn't give me an X-ray. They really don't do that anymore."

He didn't give you an X-ray? A patient who suffers from asthma, with a medical record that pointed to a susceptibility to pneumonia, and the doctor hadn't *required* an X-ray! The doctor also knew about Erin's family history of cancer. Her mother had survived breast cancer, only to die ten years later at age sixty-nine from ovarian cancer.

Warning bells started ringing in my head.

"Erin, I want you to call this doctor and schedule an appointment."

She called, but a nurse informed her that the doctor was out of the clinic, sick with a head cold. I told Erin to ask for his home number. He answered and said he would write a prescription for antibiotics. He told her, "That should take care of the chest problem."

I trusted the doctor's medical expertise and opinion. I also trusted Erin. Having experienced a myriad of medical problems in the past, she said—as a healer—she knew how to take care of herself.

I uneasily shifted my concern for her health to the back of my mind. Yet, she didn't feel well enough to resume our morning walks.

December: We bought an eight-foot Christmas tree and spent the next two days decorating, not only the tree but the outside of the house with hundreds of icicle lights, wreaths and candles. I wondered what the deer, especially the fawns, thought of this electrical spectacle.

Erin felt well enough to have a small Christmas party; she wanted to show off the decorations. We scheduled a stand-up, wine and hors 'd oeuvre party for December 10th and invited twenty new friends and neighbors. Although fatigued at the end of the evening, Erin seemed to be doing okay. A winter storm decorated the trees with fluffy snow and covered the ground in white. We frolicked in the snow like silly kids.

Then, our idyllic world changed.

I received an e-mail informing me that Time Warner had decided to close up their on-line writing experiment on December 15. The production of *Polo Wives* was cancelled. "Sorry," my editor told me on the phone.

Click

Erin and I had planned a weekend stay in a local resort on December 18 to celebrate our first wedding anniversary. Three days before we were to depart she couldn't get out of bed. She could hardly breathe. "You better cancel our honeymoon reservation," she said. That trip meant a lot to her. Something was desperately wrong.

I called the doctor. "My wife's condition is worsening," I said. "I want to bring her in to see you."

He scoffed. "That won't be necessary. I'm treating her for pneumonia. The antibiotics will do it."

Pneumonia! Over the phone! What kind of quack was this guy? That did it. On December 22, I took Erin to the clinic as a walk-in patient to see another doctor. Any other doctor.

Erin had been in the new doctor's office for an hour—I was beginning to get edgy—when she finally emerged. She looked frightened. "You'd better come back with me," she said hesitantly. "The doctor wants to show you something."

I shook hands with the doctor, a large man with huge hands. Erin sat on the examination table. The doctor didn't smile as he said, "You wife tells me that two months ago she could walk about a mile. Now she can only walk from room to room before she gets shortness of breath."

"That's true," I answered. "It was almost two months ago when she stopped our daily walks."

"Her medical chart states that she is being treated for pneumonia"—The doctor cocked his head—"with antibiotics?"

"For almost a month," I answered, feeling helpless. Why hadn't I done something about this stupid telephone treatment before!

He continued, "She also told me that she's had pain in her left shoulder over the last few weeks and has been seeing a chiropractor and a massage person."

"Yes." *Where was he going with this?*

His face took on a grim look. "I feel it is far more serious than that. She has a lump, here, on her neck." He showed me. "I'm going to set your wife up with an X-ray immediately."

"Then this could be serious," I said.

The doctor's demeanor turned stoic, but I saw sadness in his eyes, as if he wanted to say, "I'm sorry." Instead, he said, "The X-ray will answer that question."

An hour later Erin and I looked at the chest X-ray in disbelief. The plate looked like a night photograph of a snowstorm, the falling snow blurred in the camera's flash. There was a large "snowball" on her left lung that appeared more ominous than the rest.

The elderly doctor who'd examined the X-ray glanced at Erin as he took the X-ray off the viewing screen, nodded his head, and with a forlorn look backed away.

I hugged Erin, smelling the sweet perfume on her cheek, which helped mask the clinic's antiseptic odor. A dying fly buzzed fitfully on the floor.

I turned to Erin and looked into her terrified eyes. We didn't say the words to each other, but I knew what she was thinking, what we *both* were thinking:

Cancer.

Erin was immediately scheduled for a cat scan, which showed the disease had spread to her liver and kidneys. Another doctor took a biopsy of her left lung and drained that lung of fluid. While Erin recovered from the effects of the biopsy, I talked to the doctor, a matronly woman with a face of stone.

"You wife has stage four cancer. It's extremely serious."

"Is it something that can be treated?" I asked, hearing the pleading tone in my own voice.

The doctor shook her head.

"Could it be treated enough to go in remission?" Now I was begging.

"No, it can't." She shrugged. As I looked at her, I had the gut feeling that she was thinking, *It's not my problem. She's not my patient.* "What you wife has is incurable. In my estimation, she has no more than a month to live."

I stood there, trembling, my world, Erin's world, *our* world was flickering like a candle in the wind. My eyes welled with tears, but I didn't cry. Not then, not in front of this bleak doctor who offered no hope for the survival of my wife. I hissed, "Don't you tell my wife."

The doctor nodded, spun on her clunky heel, and left me alone. I found an exit and walked outside into the cold night air. Tears began to pour down my cheeks. I raised my arms to the darkening sky and screamed, "Goddamn you to hell, *God!* Goddamn you! You can't take this vibrant girl. Take *me*, you bastard!" I ranted on and on, yelling at a vacant, uncaring cold sky, screaming at a bloodless God. Weak and limp from emotion, I stopped my tirade.

I can do something. I can find a way to treat Erin. I will find a way.

Yes!

When I drove Erin home that night she was tipsy, a little drunk on the vile liquid she had to consume for the biopsy. At least, she didn't think about the cancer. As I tucked the covers around her neck, and before she fell asleep, she mumbled, "Maybe it's a fungus infection."

I saw no hope in that.

The next day, the doctor at the clinic called and said they were setting up a room in the Virginia Mason Hospital in Seattle for further examination. Erin was dozing on the couch, so I walked into the back bedroom to talk to the doctor. I said, "I was told how serious this is."

I could hear his deep sigh. "We have little hope."

"Do me one favor, doctor. Tomorrow is Christmas Eve, let us share the joy of that day, and Christmas day, before we go to the hospital."

"Of course, another day or two won't make—" He stopped abruptly.

I gritted my teeth. "Don't tell my wife *any* of this."

Five minutes later Erin's primary physician, the *telephone* doctor, called offering his sympathy and asking if there was anything he could do. I wanted to scream, "You killed my wife, you bastard!" but I hung up instead. I would never hear from him again.

I told Erin we were going to the Seattle hospital for more tests, perhaps treatment. I wanted her to try and relax. First, I explained, we'd have Christmas together at home. She nodded wearily.

I eased her down on a living room couch, tucked a blanket around her, and stretched out on the other couch. The two couches were positioned in an "L" shape so our heads were only a few feet apart. I couldn't sleep; my mind was in turmoil. It was as though thousands of electrical flashes were darting through my skull.

After a few minutes, Erin said in a soft, almost ethereal voice, "I know you're there."

I turned my head to look at her. Her eyes were closed.

"I know you're there," she repeated. "I can feel you pressing on the cushion."

I was still on my couch.

I slipped to the floor, crawled the few feet to her. "I didn't touch you."

Her eyes opened and she smiled. "Then it's my angel. She came to me twice." She saw the tears on my cheeks and wiped them away with her fingertips. "Do not be afraid," she said. "I am now protected."

On Christmas Eve we opened our presents. We tried so hard to be happy. Through a veil of tears, I said, "I love you soooo much. Merry . . . Christmas."

"Yes, Christmas, and in the last few days I've been poked a lot with needles. I feel like a pincushion. And now I'm having a glass of wine, then I'll have another, enough to make me feel that I don't care about anything."

"And next, we're going to open Christmas presents. Do you love me?"

"More than the world, Clay."

"That's impossible, because I love *you* more that the world."

We unwrapped the Christmas presents. She gave me tennis clothes, and I gave her a large statue of Santa Claus that had a tag on it that read, "Love, prosperity and long life."

We stopped and stared at each other. Although we didn't say it, we both felt we would not even have one year. Perhaps, only a month. We continued opening presents, saving a few for Christmas Day.

In the morning I was surprised to see that Erin was feeling well enough to prepare Eggs Benedict for our breakfast. I opened a bottle of champagne.

Erin tasted the bubbly wine. "Whoopee!" she said, before downing the glass. She had on a terrycloth robe. On it she wore the button I had given her on Christmas Eve, which proclaimed, "The World's Cutest Leprechaun."

We laughed through a film of Christmas tears.

The next day I drove Erin to the dock where we boarded the ferry to Seattle. Once in the hospital room, a doctor, who had the standard grim look pasted on his face, met us.

"Your records have been mailed FedEx. We should have them shortly."

That was it, no words of encouragement. When he left, Erin said, "Looks like they've put me in a black bag and are ready to zip it closed."

The nurses bought in a rickety fold-up bed, saying I could stay overnight. Neither Erin nor I slept well; every hour or so a nurse came in and took Erin's vital signs, temperature, blood pressure and pulse.

The next morning an oncologist, a cancer specialist, dropped by. Although he seemed apathetic, he gave us a glimmer of hope. Erin had told me the night before she'd decided she would not go through chemotherapy. She had watched her mother die horribly, vomiting daily from the treatment.

The oncologist said, "Chemotherapy is far easier to tolerate than when your mother underwent the treatment."

"What are my odds?" Erin asked.

"Well, I haven't seen your records, but I'd guess about fifty-fifty."

Guess! I held Erin's hand tightly, asking her, "Would you take the chance?"

Softly: "Yes."

The second day, another nameless doctor appeared to check on Erin. He was young, but at least he was sympathetic. What he said was not consoling. "We, ah, seem to have lost your records. Well, not lost them, but they were sent by regular mail, not FedEx. We may not get them until after the holidays."

Incensed, I demanded, "Why didn't someone hand carry them? Hell, I could have picked them up and brought them."

"I'm sorry," the young doctor said, backing out of the room. I had learned that doctors like to back away from patients, like ghosts fading into the mist.

Erin dictated a list of all her personal items, and the persons or relatives who would receive the bequests. She signed it, and I witnessed the hand-written document. I felt as if another door had closed.

The third day: The young doctor returned to report that Erin's records still hadn't arrived. I told him we would wait one more day. To Erin, I said, "We're getting out of this place."

This tomb, I thought.

The next morning, the news was the same—no records. I stared the young physician in the eyes, daring him to break eye contact, to back away. "Doctor, I want you to release my wife from this hospital. If you don't, I'm going to carry her out of here and no force is going to stop me. We're going to a place where I can get my wife treated."

I had made a decision, and Erin had agreed. We would pack up immediately and make the three-day drive to Santa Barbara to the cancer center.

As the young doctor once again backed out of Erin's hospital room, he said, "I'll sign the release papers."

I drove Erin home and started to tear apart the Christmas decorations, ripping and cutting the wires to the tree and outdoor lights, throwing everything away. I saved the Christmas ornaments that had been hand-made by Erin's mother.

The next morning, I packed our clothes (dear Erin was terribly sick, but tried to help, sitting in a chair, directing me what to take of hers), and by early afternoon we were ready. I made a nest of pillows for Erin in the right seat of the Subaru. We drove away.

We knew not what the future held for us, but we were reaching out, desperate for help.

For hope.

Chapter 21

Celebration of Life

We spent New Year's Eve at a Day's Inn motel about fifty miles south of Portland. I had driven five hours. Erin slept most of the time, comfortable in the cocoon of pillows. I purchased a bag full of chicken, potatoes, gravy and cold slaw from a Kentucky Fried Chicken next door to the motel. The chicken was too greasy to eat, so we made do with the mashed potatoes and gravy. As Erin slept quietly, I opened a bottle of wine, thinking wistfully about the Princess cruise ship on which we'd planned to celebrate a Caribbean New Year's.

Two days later, in a lashing rain, and after twenty-two hours of intense driving, we arrived in Santa Barbara. It was almost 5:00 PM when I checked into an Extended Stay suite, which had a small kitchen. We had no other place to go. We had booked the beach apartment for mid-January, two weeks away.

After checking into Extended Stay, we immediately went to see my primary physician whom I'd contacted before we departed Washington. We arrived just as he was ministering to his last patient of the day. He shook my hand, and I introduced him to Erin, who looked ashen with fatigue. I could see her hands trembling; I took them in mine to calm her. The doctor said he'd made an appointment for us for the next day with the "best cancer specialist" in Santa Barbara. "We are going to treat your wife's cancer aggressively," he added.

Aggressively!

These were the words I had been waiting to hear, so unlike the gloomy, impotent doctors at the Seattle hospital.

The next morning we met with the oncologist, Dr. Susan Hart, at the Santa Barbara Cancer Center. A tall, angular, no-nonsense woman, she said, "I see cancer patients every day. The disease is not a mystery to me, nor do I fear it as other doctors do." She looked at Erin who sat up straight, eyes wide with hope. "Erin, your cancer is incurable, but that doesn't mean you can't have life, a good quality life. You are a young, strong woman. I will treat your cancer aggressively."

Yes!

That night Erin and I held each other tightly, knowing that, perhaps, just perhaps, there was a chance for life. Although we already felt like we had lived a lifetime with the disease, it was the most reassured we'd felt since that life-shattering day in December.

December 22, only two weeks earlier.

The following morning I made up Erin's pillow cocoon and drove her to the cancer center for her first chemotherapy treatment. She voiced her fears to me, admitting her terror that she would react to the chemotherapy as her mother had.

The nurse settled Erin in a huge sofa chair with a tubular, stainless steel stand to clip on the plastic intravenous bottles. There were five other patients in the room, resting quietly in sofa chairs, all of them in their seventies and eighties. One man looked at youthful Erin and smiled sadly.

Seeing Erin's nervousness, the nurse tried to calm her fears. "Chemotherapy has come a long way in the last ten years. We can control the sickness."

Erin managed a weak smile.

This first chemotherapy session lasted five hours. I took Erin to our hotel, not knowing what to expect.

She slept.

She slept the next day for twenty hours, then the day after that for another twenty. I didn't wake her, just watched over her: She looked peaceful, serene. Each day, when she finally stirred, I fed her spoonfuls of chicken-noodle soup that I made in our tiny motel kitchen. It would be two weeks before her next treatment.

I took morning walks, calling it my thinking time. I needed to figure out what we were going to do, where we were going to live. We still had our home in Port Townsend, but I knew we would never return there to live. We couldn't go to the beach apartment we'd rented. Located on the second floor of the building, the apartment had two floors, the bedrooms upstairs. Erin couldn't climb the stairs.

Then I thought of a possible a solution, or at least I hoped I had—the polo condominium my ex-wife and I still owned. She had remarried and moved into her new husband's home. We had already agreed to rent the condo and share the proceeds. I hadn't talked to her for several weeks so I had no idea if it had been rented. With my heart in my throat, I called her.

"This is Clay, I'm in Santa Barbara."

"Yes." Her reply was guarded.

"Have you rented the condo?"

"No. I placed the ad for a month but no takers."

I breathed a sigh of relief. "Can I rent it?"

Silence. Then I broke down. I blurted, "Erin has cancer."

"Oh, God," I heard her say. I knew that her new husband had lost two wives to cancer. She understood a little about the hell a spouse goes through.

I struggled to contain my emotions. "It's . . . it's incurable. She's going through chemotherapy. We don't know how long she will live. I'd . . . we'd like to rent the condo?"

"I'll have to think about it." After a few more words, she hung up. I didn't know what to expect.

She called an hour later and agreed.

When I told Erin, she nodded her head. I knew she felt no joy at the prospect of living in a place formerly occupied by a woman who hated her.

Erin went for another chemotherapy session, the second out of a series of seven. This time she actually looked forward to it, realizing the medicines being pumped into her veins were breathing life into her. Once she recovered from the second chemo session, she began to walk more steadily.

On February 2nd, almost five weeks after we arrived in Santa Barbara, we moved into the blank walls and empty space of the polo condo. We purchased a bedroom set and sofa. It was a start. I tape-recorded my thoughts:

Erin has gone through two chemotherapy sessions and she is feeling better, constantly better. She is able to do things now, she can walk, and can even answer e-mail on her laptop. We have great hope for the future, especially after the second cat scan. We were both terrified to learn the results. On February twenty-second (exactly two months after the initial cancer diagnosis), Dr. Hart called us on the telephone and left this message:

"Hey you two, Dr. Hart calling. The cat scan looks great! Everything is significantly improved and I couldn't have wished for better. So we'll go ahead with the same treatments—and you're doing good! I'll see you then."

We held each other for a long time as we let the words, "significantly improved," and, "couldn't have wished for better," comfort us.
Erin had life!

Erin made an appointment at the hairdressers to buy a wig and found one close to the same color and style as her real hair. Then, she made another appointment to have her head shaved. She hadn't started to lose her hair, but hated the idea of it falling out in clumps.

With a grin, Erin told me the story. "I sat in the beauty chair and there were two women on either side of me when the hairdresser began to shave my head with an electric razor. The women were aghast. One of them asked, "Isn't that a bit extreme?"

I took Erin to Nordstrom department store where she purchased half a dozen wide-brimmed hats, berets, scarves and billed caps.

On the 26th of February, Erin went for her third chemotherapy. She almost skipped into the cancer center. I thought she was going to shout to the other patients, "I'm going to live!" Had she done so, I would have joined in on the chorus.

In between each session, Erin had to take a series of five injections to keep her white blood cell count normal. These caused her extreme distress. The first one almost dropped her to her knees. I had to hold her steady, but she didn't utter a word of distress.

During this time, I began to teach my writing classes again. I also started a major rewrite on *To Be or Not To Be Shakespeare*, which the mystery editor at Time Warner had asked me to do before the iPublish project was cancelled. Writing became my personal form of therapy. I hadn't written one word since the previous December. *What will I do with the novel now*? I wondered. *Let it collect dust?* I wasn't in the right mental state to market it.

I wanted Erin to go back to writing *The Goddess Spot*, but she said that she wasn't ready. Instead, she e-mailed her long list of friends, updating them on her progress. She decided to buy a Celtic harp, as she wanted to continue with the lessons she had started a year earlier in Santa Barbara. We bought two harps, a large concert one, and the half-size Celtic harp. She fussed over the harps, tuning them as if they were her children.

March 19th: Chemotherapy #4.

We celebrated Easter by going to the services at the Santa Barbara Mission, then to our favorite place, The El Encanto Hotel, high on the Riviera, for Sunday Brunch. Erin reacted badly to the champagne—she hadn't had a glass of wine since our arrival in Santa Barbara—so we left the restaurant early. She said, "Okay, no wine for me, at least for a while."

April 9th. Chemotherapy #5.

By this time, Erin was known to all the nurses and doctors in the cancer center. Her exuberance for life was infectious. When she'd walk down the hall, everyone commented, "Oh, you look so good!"

April 30th. Chemotherapy #6.

Erin was exhausted after this last chemotherapy. Although the medicine seemed to beat down most of the cancer cells, it was taking a toll on her body.

We told the doctor that we needed to travel to our home in Port Townsend and move our personal things to Santa Barbara. We had decided to put the house up for sale. The hard part would be getting our two cars back to Santa Barbara. Previously, with the doctor's approval, I had let Erin drive the Subaru around Santa Barbara. She did fine. But could she drive the twenty–two hours from Washington?

"Sure, I can," she answered.

Bulldog, I thought. But it worried me.

With Dr. Hart's blessing—much to Erin's relief—she okayed holding off on the seventh chemotherapy until our return to Santa Barbara—we flew to Seattle and took a shuttle bus to our house. It was tough walking into our enchanted cottage in the forest, knowing that the two weeks we would be spending there would be our last. Those weeks were spent in a frenzy of packing and planning. Erin worked hard and I watched her carefully.

We advertised the sale of our furniture, except Erin's baby grand piano, and my desk, then had a huge two-day garage sale. By the time it was over and the movers had come and gone we were looking at an empty home. Our enchanted cottage had become a sad, cold dwelling. We saved the last day to pack the two cars with our clothes.

That day, Erin woke up sick.

She'd had a relapse and couldn't get out of bed. "I'll be okay," she said, "I just need a full-day's rest."

I was nervous and worried. What if she couldn't drive? I began to make contingency plans in my head. Maybe I could rent a U-Haul trailer for one of the cars. Could the BMW pull another car? Should I call her son and fly him up here? *Why didn't I think of this earlier?*

The next morning, Erin awoke, her eyes clear, her vibrancy back. "I can do it," she said.

She drove her BMW. I set up headlight signals in case she had problems. Driving away from our home, I wondered it I had done the right thing. What if Erin collapsed while we were in transit to Santa Barbara? Was I asking too much of her?

I watched her car though the rear view mirror more than I did the highway. After five hours of driving, I noticed her headlights blinking rapidly, the signal to pull off the highway. Just ahead I saw an off ramp and several motel signs.

"Whew," she said as we got out of the cars. "That's all I could drive today. I was starting to ache all over and began dozing off."

Only three more five-hour driving days left, I thought. Deep in my heart, I didn't think she would make it.

But my worries were unfounded, Erin never had another problem.

"See, I told you I was a bulldog," she said after we completed the third day's drive. On the last day, we rolled into Santa Barbara with ease.

May 20th: Erin went in for her seventh chemotherapy, the last of the series. After a cat scan indicated traces of cancer in her liver and kidneys, Dr. Hart decided to start a new series of chemotherapy treatments using a different drug.

"Looks like I'm going to have to do this all my life," Erin said. "But it's better than not having a life." In June she had two treatments with the new drug.

On July 9th: I made an entry in my daily calendar: ERIN SHAVED HER LEGS! She also began to grow peach fuzz on her head.

Polo season had started in Santa Barbara, and I took Erin to the clubhouse for Sunday brunch and introduced her to dozens of friends. We went to the games every weekend during July and August.

"I want to have a party on our terrace," Erin said one day, "and invite all the new friends I have met since we've been at the polo fields."

"Good idea, let's do it."

"I'll call it *A Celebration of Life.*"

At the gathering of thirty guests, Erin wore a romantic ankle-length dress and sunbonnet. During the party, I made an announcement that Erin was undergoing treatment for cancer, which only a few people knew. We all toasted to her and to *life.*

Soon after, I received a note from my ex-wife. It was written on the anniversary of our wedding.

Clay,
Since it's anniversary time, I had been thinking about a note to you. Just wanted to let you know that if I had to do it all over again, even knowing the ending, I would have chosen you. Thanks for the good years.
I can't even imagine what you're going through. My husband, knows exactly how you feel, he lost two wives to cancer. I have my miracle. Hope you get yours.

I stared at the letter for a long time, especially the word *miracle*.

Erin underwent two more chemotherapy sessions, then one big scare. Her shoulders had started to ache terribly. Although Erin had passed her mammogram test without a hitch, this new development worried Dr. Hart. She ordered a scan for bone cancer.

Bone cancer!

We had come so far! Erin couldn't have bone cancer. When the bone cancer scan showed nothing, we were both limp with relief. I told Erin I felt like we had taken a ride on a roller coaster and would never get off. Dr. Hart prescribed morphine pills for Erin's back pain, which I didn't like as she was already on a dozen other pills as well as her asthma inhalers. The doctor also prescribed a second, higher dosage morphine in case of severe pain.

Morphine, I thought. *Morphine for severe pain.*

Then came the big one. No, not a problem with cancer— a trip to Cancun, Mexico on the Yucatan Peninsula. I had received an offer from the Paradisus Riviera Cancun, an all-inclusive resort hotel, to stay for three nights

"I can't believe it, we're going to Cancun!" Erin had stars in her eyes. "I was there ten years ago. I want to write my third book about the Mayans." She eyed me like, *Look out, what you're about to hear may turn you off.* "No, don't say anything, but I believe I was reincarnated as a Mayan Priestess who lived in the year 800 AD."

"No problem," I said. "I'll bet you had long black hair."

"Yes, and I wore a peacock feathered headdress."

"And a low-cut clinging gown?"

She put her arms around me and crushed a kiss to my lips, then said, "When I wore it, the gown shimmered in the sun."

As you shimmer now, I thought.

Chapter 22

Life Is So Precious

We flew to Cancun in early September for a ten-day stay and checked into the 500-room Paridisus Riviera Cancun, which is—as the hotel brochure says—an ultra inclusive service resort. We were issued colored plastic wristbands, which saved us the bother of signing restaurant bills or paying tips. With the wristband, we could enjoy all meals, snacks, liquor and wine, entertainment and sports facilities. The Spa was extra, but Erin enjoyed several much-needed massages. It was like being on a cruise ship, one that never leaves the dock.

There was a huge pool near the beach. "It's a lagoon," Erin said.

Over the next few days, I'd watch her gazing at the beach. "I love this," she said each day as we relaxed on lounge chairs.

"I feel like I can live forever!" she'd add.

A few days later, she remarked, "Life is so precious."

We sipped Pina Coladas, waded in the shoulder-deep lagoon, holding tightly to each other. And we made love, the first time in eight months.

After three days and nights, I rented a car for the four-hour drive to the Mayan ruins at Uxmal, the site Erin had visited ten years earlier. Or was it 1,200 years ago?

I wrote Erin's story this way:

"The light . . ." I heard my wife, Erin, say in a hushed, reverent tone. "It's brilliant."

I stuck my head out of the stone doorway of the House of Turtles, shading my eyes from the intensity of the midday sun. "Yeah, sun's not only bright, it's hot." The temperature at the Mayan ruins in Uxmal (pronounced *oosh*-MAHL) in Yucatan, Mexico, was over 90 degrees. My sweat-soaked shirt stuck to my skin like a wet rag, courtesy of the intense humidity.

"No, not the sun," Erin said, still staring into the dim chamber of the House of Turtles.

I craned my neck to look above me at the frieze of carved stone turtles, which seemed to march around the four sides of the small, flat-topped temple.

Then I looked at Erin, who still stared into the dim chamber.

"I saw a flash of brilliant light." She pointed. "In that chamber."

I stuck my head inside the stone doorway and sniffed. "I smell urine."

She stretched her arm forward, passing her fingers through the portal into the empty chamber. I got the feeling she was reaching into another dimension, like in the movie *Stargate*.

Erin turned back and squinted into the sun. "The Mayans had the ability to turn into light, to travel into another dimension. The one I saw—"

"Did he, ah, she . . . um, *it*, have a body?" I asked.

"No, just the light, as if he'd come from a parallel world." She turned to look me. "The Mayans believed there was another world that ran parallel to their own, one in another dimension."

She started walking toward the nearby Pyramid of the

Magician, which rose 114 feet above the dense forest. I
followed, passing several iguanas sunning themselves on a pile
of rocks. I stepped into the shadow of the pyramid to escape the
sun. There were dozens of people in brightly colored shirts
scaling the steep, stone stairway to the top of the pyramid. In
place of the tourists, I envisioned Mayan priests in multi-
colored ceremonial robes and feathered headdresses, their necks
adorned with jade and obsidian necklaces—
    And I saw Erin wearing a shimmering white, flowing
robe.
    I blinked, and shook my head. The image faded. I
looked at Erin as she stood beside me, attired in shorts, sneakers
and a damp T-shirt. "Uh, this might surprise you, I saw a—" I
gulped and said rapidly, "I saw a vision of you in a white robe
and a headdress of—"
    "Peacock feathers," she said. She took my hand in hers.
    "It was years ago when I first started having dreams
about this place. I saw the different temples, the hieroglyphs,
and the paintings, the people—and myself. I wore a peacock
headdress." She touched her throat. "Around my neck I wore a
jeweled necklace of jade. I was regal and was invited to the
ceremonies, saw the priests. The Mayans had wonderful healing
voices and a healing energy that came through their hands. They
were clairvoyant and able to see both the past and the future.
Through their visions and the precision of their astronomical
knowledge they could predict the future." She rubbed a stone on
the cornice of the Pyramid of the Magician. "This is my place.
    "This is my time."

    After three days of climbing over Mayan ruins (Erin was

like a mountain goat, never tiring), we returned to the Paridisus Riviera resort to catch our flight home. At the airport in Cancun, I pointed out to Erin a tall, attractive woman with pixie-cut hair, not any longer than Erin's new growth of hair. Erin took off her hat and for the next two weeks she never wore it again. She loved her "fuzzy" hair.

The day after we got back, Erin had another chemotherapy treatment. A week later, yet another. The doctor seemed to be making up for lost time. But at the same time, Erin grew weak from the treatments. She began to slow her pace; tears came freely and often to her eyes.

One day Dr. Hart called us into her office and closed the door behind us. She had never done that before. Erin looked at me, and I saw the fear in her eyes. The doctor advised she was putting Erin on a new treatment, one less severe. "We'll see how it works."

Outside the office, Erin collapsed against my body. "I thought that was it," she said. "When she closed the door, I felt like I was in a vacuum, and she was going to say, 'Too bad, we tried.' "

As we walked away arm in arm, I thought, *The doctor knows something we don't know, but won't tell us.* I felt a sliver of fear go through me like an icicle piercing my heart.

Erin put more energy into her self-healing process.

She had fought hard during the last ten months, calling upon everything she knew as a healer the cure the cancer. She had taken acupuncture (until the needles began to leave huge bruises), used massages, read a myriad of books on healing and special diets. She had two friends who were healers and she contacted them by e-mail for support and knowledge. She had a small circular, pewter labyrinth and each night she would run a special pencil through its grooves. Her silver rosary was always at her side and she prayed to God, to the Virgin Mary, and to her special angel.

But the chemotherapy kept dragging her down.

She told me. "I don't think I can take any more." She shuddered. "My body and mind are a wreck." We talked to the doctor, expressing our feelings.

"I'm reluctant to take you off the treatments as they are helping," she said. "But if this one isn't working, I'll try another."

Erin said, "In Cancun, I felt I had a life, a quality of life. I would rather have that for a short time than quantity of life and feel terrible each day."

The doctor nodded impassively.

I interjected, "We have the opportunity to go to Northern Ireland for a week on October the first." The travel association, of which I was a member, had set up a media trip for twenty-five members and spouses to go to Ireland for a week, visiting Dublin, Belfast, and County Down, the birthplace of Erin's ancestors. She desperately wanted to take the trip.

"I have to go," she told the doctor, "even if it's the last thing I do in my life."

Dr. Hart smiled. "I have no problem with that. We'll work on a new treatment regimen when you get back."

I wondered whether the doctor was giving Erin a lease on life—or a lease on time.

It was a twelve-hour flight to Dublin, but Erin managed it without serious problems. Yet, she tired easily. On the second night in Belfast, after a long day tour, she didn't have the energy to go to dinner, so I ordered room service.

Then it happened.

It was about one in the morning. We were both asleep when the room phone rang. Erin answered and told me they wanted the room service tray put in the hallway.

I started to get up, but she said she'd take it. I was too groggy to object. I heard the door open, and then a crash and a cry from Erin. I rushed out the door to see her sprawled on the hallway carpet, the service dishes scattered around her. Before I knew it two security people were there. I told then to go away, that I could handle the situation.

When they didn't move, I blurted, "I'd like to know whose goddamn idea it was to wake us in the early morning for a damn tray!" I was livid. Before I punched someone, I picked up Erin and carried her back to the bed.

"You think you're okay?" I asked after I slammed the door. "I can call a doctor."

"I don't know what happened," she said, breathing hard. "I just blacked-out."

I felt her body, but found nothing broken.

The next morning she walked with a limp. "I must have bruised myself," she said, her shoulder's sagging.

The rest of the trip was uneventful. Although she continued to limp—she tried to hide it from the others—she went to every event, not wanting to miss any of Ireland. Especially the trip to Down Patrick.

After we discovered her ancestor's tomb, she announced her contentment. "I'm ready to leave." She gripped my hand. "I need Doctor Hart's help."

The twelve-hour flight back to California seemed to go on forever. Something was wrong, terribly wrong.

Dr. Hart gave Erin one more chemotherapy treatment and ordered a brain scan. The diagnosis: Erin had several brain tumors. She was immediately scheduled for a series of fifteen radiation treatments, five each week.

Erin and I never discussed this new development; perhaps we were too stunned to react. But we both knew that yet another obstacle had been placed in her pathway to life.

Yet, the treatments seemed to work. They were painless and over in a few minutes. Erin got over her limp. The thing she didn't get over was the loss of hair on her head. The radiation burned it off. She would look wistfully in the mirror at her bare head, but she didn't cry. Never complained. I knew she could endure whatever happened.

I wasn't sure I could.

Yet, in a terrible and strange way, I felt something I had never felt before. I was helping to save Erin's life. I was spending every waking moment with her, caring for her. I willed myself to be strong. Erin called me her, "Knight in Shining Armor."

The Public Relations woman for the Delta Queen Steamboat Company sent an e-mail offering a trip over Thanksgiving.

"Want to go back on the Delta Queen?" I asked Erin.

Her answer was typically Erin. She pouted. "I can't get into my red sequined dress." Because of the chemotherapy treatments and the injections, Erin had gained twenty-five pounds, a side effect that irked her, especially since she was eating little. She so loved her dresses, and hated the extra weight.

"Order more dresses," I said. She loved to shop on-line. For the next month something arrived at the door almost daily. Not all of them fit and had to be returned. But it made Erin happy to try on new clothes. She was still a woman.

Ten days before we departed for New Orleans, Erin developed a hacking cough. Dr. Hart ordered a chest X-ray. The large tumor in her chest had returned. Once again, radiation treatments were scheduled. She underwent four treatments before our departure to New Orleans. We talked to the radiation doctor about the trip. He replied, "No, I don't think it's a good idea." Then he saw the look on Erin's face. "Well, what difference does it make. Of course, you can go."

Although I worried about the "What difference does it make," I pushed away my negative thoughts.

Erin was happy on the Delta Queen as we relived our adventure of four years earlier when she wore the shimmering red dress on New Year's. Then, we hadn't had a care in the world. We giggled, remembering her episode on the street in New Orleans with the Ben Wa balls. Each morning, we walked a mile on the steamboat's deck, climbing up and down ladders for extra exercise. Erin felt great.

We are still going to beat this treacherous bastard called cancer, I told myself.

Erin resumed the radiation treatments when got back. Dr. Hart was ready to serve up more chemotherapy treatments when the radiation was done.

It was then that Erin began to have problems with her speech and her ability to write legibly. She stopped using the computer and her limp returned. She had difficulty climbing the eight steps at the entryway to our condo.

"I want a cane," she said.

"Hey," I answered, "you have me, a good strong arm."

"I may need a cane." She brushed my cheek with her lips. "Clay, I want you to do one thing for me."

I was thinking about how I would get her a cane when she surprised me by saying, "I want you to take me to Catalina so we can celebrate our second wedding anniversary."

On December 17th we arrived at the ferry departure landing. I let Erin out and went to park the car. When I returned, several people stood around her. I heard a woman ask, "You sure you're all right?"

I hurried to Erin. "What happened?"

"I don't know. I just collapsed and fell under the front of a car. Some people pulled me away before it ran over me."

Oh, God, no, don't let this happen, not now. Give us these few days.

We were granted those two days. Erin had difficulty climbing the circular staircase to our room, but my arm steadied her. We celebrated our anniversary with champagne and held each other tightly as if forever would never come.

When we got back, Erin created a computer Christmas card for my daughter. In it she wrote:

December 21, 2002   Christmas

I couldn't let this holiday go by without celebrating and appreciating your kind expressions throughout the year – whether it's an "I hope you are feeling better" or something nice to your Dad like pictures of the grandbabies (cute, by the way!). I know how difficult it has been for you, but I am also acutely aware of how soothing it is for your Dad. He loves all of you very much.
Merry Christmas and
God's blessings
Erin

These were the last words Erin wrote, a cry to be part of the family, and an attempt to seal a bond between my daughter and me.

We celebrated Christmas, I gave Erin pearl earrings with inset diamonds. She gave me a three-foot-high silver-armored knight. "You will always be my Knight in Shining Armor."

Then her green eyes brightened and she said something strange. "I see in you a shining soul." It was if she had seen into another world. The Otherworld.

The day after Christmas, Erin had another cat scan and a lung biopsy. We were going through the motions and following doctor's orders.

Invited to a friend's beach home for a New Year's party, Erin dressed in a new gown she had just got in the mail. I told her she looked like the Queen of the Prom.

January 2nd: My daughter, husband and two children visited for a belated Christmas. Erin spent the day with her son. Sadly, my daughter, even after the card she had received, did not want to see Erin. When my daughter was ready to leave, I said, "Erin is dying." The tears started to come, muffling my next words: "You never got to meet her, to know her."

January 3-4th: Erin is unsteady and sleeps till noon.

Sunday, January 5th: Erin asked me to take her to the Mission for mass. She wore black.

At the church I let her out of the car—stupidly!—to find a parking place. Less than a minute later I saw a group of people crowding around her fallen body. A woman was bending over her. When I identified myself as her husband, she replied, "I'm a nurse. She had a bad fall, but her eyes are fine, there is no concussion."

I got Erin to her feet and the crowd dispersed. I felt her head; there was a knot on the back of her skull.

Oh, my poor, sweet Erin.

She couldn't climb the steps to the mission, so I took her home. She had missed her final visit with God in God's house.

I began to think about God. I wanted to curse him for taking away such a young, beautiful, talented woman who had so much to live for. Instead, I thanked him.

Thank you, God, for letting me wake up to see Erin beside me.

January 6: Sunday morning 2:00 AM.

Erin woke up screaming and crying that she had terrible pains all over her body. For the first time, I gave her two emergency morphine pills. The pain didn't lessen. I gave her two more. Finally, in a drugged state, she fell asleep. I decided I had to take her to the hospital.

Early the next morning, I called her son, Brett, and told him what had happened. "We must to take your mother to the hospital." I paused. "It's time."

I called a nurse who set up a room in the cancer ward, then I awakened Erin and told her I had to take her to the hospital for tests.

"Anything you want to take along?" I asked.

"You."

At the hospital she was put in a wheelchair, then we fought through the nit-picking process of checking in. "What are we doing here?" Erin asked, confused, her mind blurred by the morphine.

"Just checking you in for the tests and treatment."

She had to sign the admissions paper, which she did with difficulty, a labored scrawl, nothing like her delicate signature

After Erin was settled into hospital room, Dr. Hart came by. Her son and I met with her in the hallway. "How much time does she have?" I asked, forcing the words through gritted teeth.

She held up one finger. "A week."

I breathed out, couldn't seem to breathe in. I heard her son sob next to my shoulder.

The doctor continued. "Erin is on intravenous morphine and tranquilizers. She will be given no food, nor will the nurses take vital signs."

She will starve to death, I thought.

As if reading my thoughts, the doctor said, "She will go quietly and not suffer any pain."

Dr. Hart left. Brett and I embraced. I told him I felt that one week was the outside. "I don't believe she will live more than a few days."

"I have to arrange for the Last Rights," he said, lips quivering.

The next few days Brett and I visited Erin, giving her tastes of fruit juice, and gum to chew to cleanse her mouth. With tubes in her left wrist, I'd sit on the end of the bed to be as close to her as I could. There I could look at her face, her pale face, the green eyes no longer bright. I'd read her jokes from the *Reader's Digest*, and readings from her favorite book, *Grace*. She would smile sometimes, but didn't respond. I'm sure Erin knew she was dying, but she didn't say anything. I could see it in her eyes: They were saying, *I'm sorry.*

Sorry for me.

At night, I'd go home alone, eating without hunger, tossing fitfully in bed. For the first time she wasn't next to me wanting to "huggle." I'd say to myself, *Look, God, Mr. Supreme Being, Sir! Just keep Erin alive for a few more days. I can take this pain just as long as she's alive.*

On the third day, in the late afternoon, Erin suddenly sat upright and thrust out her arms. "I have to go!" she cried. "They want me to go!" Then she settled back down. In peace.

The angels have called her, I thought with tears in my eyes.

The next day a Catholic Priest gave Erin the Last Rites. She did not respond. That evening, I hugged her—her body was so thin—and kissed her on the lips. As I rose to go, she looked at me, her eyes bright for the first time in days, and said, clearly, "I love you, Clay."

Those were her last words, a loving note that she had willed herself to say.

One last time.

The next morning her eyes were glazed, there was no life in them. I sat on the bed and held her hand. Just after noon, I heard a strange noise in her throat. I felt her pulse, then the vein on her neck. I turned to her son and said, "You better call the nurse. You mother just died. "

A half-hour later Dr. Hart arrived, touched Erin's lifeless finger, nodded her head and then excused herself.

I leaned over and kissed my dearest Erin on her cool lips.

"I love you, Erin."

Chapter 23

A Window Into the Heavens

Two days after Erin died, I wrote her obituary. I didn't want one of those, dull formula pieces of newspaper writing: She was raised in . . . went to school at . . . her family, a sister . . . cousin . . . aunt . . . I wanted something that would touch the hearts of those who knew her. These words came from *my* heart:

Erin Hardy Mills
1955 - 2003

Erin with the jade-green eyes, Erin with luster in her laughter, laughter filled with the joy of life. Erin, who created a spark of light in each person she met. She was loved by all whom had the chance to see her, touch her hand, hear her voice. Erin who played the Celtic harp, creating music like light breezes on the wind. Erin, the gifted author, whose novel, The Goddess Spot (although not completed before she died) will see fulfillment in 2003.

For Christmas 2002, I, her husband, Clay Mills, asked Santa Claus to put just one package under the tree, place it gently within the folds of the branches and wrap it in iridescent gold and silver. Let an angel watch over it. For you see this Christmas wish was a gift of life for Erin.

But a year's valiant fight with cancer finally overcame her 47-year-old heart. Erin is now with her God. She is in the hearts of her husband, and 23-year-old son. Because of our love for her she will never die.
Erin, we love you so dearly.

Erin and I had never discussed what she wanted if she died. To talk about death would have meant that we had given up hope, something we never did. Yet, while she was in the hospital, I found a note on her desk that read:

> *I want my body cremated, (wait three days so my soul can be released) and buried in a nice little plot of land with a marker so my husband and son can come and talk to me.*

At the Santa Barbara cemetery, a quiet setting that overlooks the ocean, I found such a plot in a new area that had been named the Sunrise Urn Garden. It was just what Erin would have wanted.

I also found Erin's words scratched on a letter that had come from Father Vince of the St. Barbara Parish:

> *Please have my funeral/memorial here at the Santa Barbara Mission. & please call Father Vince to do the Memorial.*

Erin had planned for her death, something she never told me. Since the parish letter was dated November 6, 2002, she must have written the note two months before she died.

Insulated by shock, living each day in a haze of unreality, I arranged for the memorial service at the Santa Barbara Mission to take place two weeks after her death. Afterward, there would be an Erin's Wake at the Sunrise Urn Garden.

At the service, Erin's ashes were placed before the altar. They were in a brass box painted in Irish green enamel with her name etched in gold on the side. I brought two dozen white roses. My daughter and son were there for the memorial services. My daughter held my hand. I didn't cry, I had cried too much in the last two weeks.

I had happened to open a children's book in Erin's desk and found this note: "To be read at my funeral." Her son had told me Erin had read the same small book at her own mother's memorial service. I asked him to read it. I had prepared something I wanted to share with the mourners. When I walked to the altar, I wasn't sure I could read through what I had written without breaking down. I started:

"For the last two years Erin and I have written
Christmas lists in lieu of New Year's resolutions.
"This last Christmas, I wrote:
"Santa, for Erin put one package under the tree,
place it gently under the branches and wrap it in
iridescent gold and silver. Let an angel watch over it.
For you see, this is a **Gift of Life** for Erin.
"And for me, Santa?
"I pray for these precious gifts: to see Erin's eyes
sparkle once again, to hear her laugh, a laugh filled with
joy, to hear her play her harp once again, just for me,
and to see her finish her novel, The Goddess Spot. But
most of all, I wish to hold her in my arms throughout
2003.

"I did hold her in my arms until that morning she died. That I will cherish forever. She is in my heart, and *will* live throughout all the years of *my* life.

"I love you, Erin."

I got through it. I had to. It was my gift of love to Erin.

At Erin's Wake, with the breeze from the ocean cool on our faces, we gathered to celebrate Erin's life. My son helped by pouring champagne, as did my daughter. Several people brought hors 'd oeuvres. There were forty chairs in a semi-circle in front of Erin's urn, and I had a harpist playing at the gravesite. The small granite headstone, embedded in the earth, said said:

Erin Hardy Mills
March 14, 1955 – January 10, 2003
I Love You

Engraved on the stone at one side was a white rose.

I had several guests read from the cards and e-mails they'd sent. Then it was over. As the people were leaving, my daughter hugged me and said, "Dad, I wish I had known Erin."

I held her warmth close for a moment and over her shoulder saw the golden light in the fading sky and the first star of the evening. I thought:

Every time God closes a door on life, he opens a window into the heavens to let the light shine down forever.

Epilogue

Somewhere In Time

Memories: The simple things I had taken for granted when Erin was alive; the smell of her clothes, the whisper of silk as she walked, the quiet fragrance of her perfume, the easy touching, the quick smile, the fan of her manicured fingers across the strings of her harp .

I am alone with these thoughts, but not totally alone.

Her spirit is always with me. I say to her, "Erin, I know you are here with every breath of air that brushes my skin, with every soft sound, a bird chirping a love song, leaves in the trees rustling together, I know the sound is you."

I began looking at the world differently—slower. I was seeing everything through two sets of eyes; Erin's and mine.

I met a psychic, a woman writer who wrote mysteries with a clairvoyant heroine. I told her about Erin and her recent death. The psychic asked, "Was she ready?"

Without thinking, I answered, "Yes," but the words bewildered me. Then I thought, *Erin prepared herself for a year to be ready. Her life, hopes and dreams may not have been fulfilled, but her call to God was the completion of her life. Yes, Erin was ready.*

Yet . . . her dreams.

It was her dream to write thirteen books, each a "gate" into the Otherworld. She had told me that her third book would take place at Uxmal, where she was once a Mayan priestess.

And the second book? When we traveled to the ancient Celtic site at Tara and New Grange just outside Dublin on our last trip to Ireland, and she had said, "Yes, this is where my next book begins." Then she grasped my hand. *"Mo ghra mo chroi."* Seeing my puzzled look, she added, "It's an ancient Celtic phrase that means, 'My love, my heart.' It can be anglicized to 'Love of my heart. ' "

"And you are the love of my life," I said.

She did hardly any writing to complete *The Goddess Spot* during her year with cancer. I learned that she had confided in her doctor that she couldn't complete the book because she knew deep in her heart that she would never be able to write another one.

I discovered her notebook in which I found 178 pages of the book with a note that she planned approximately 250 pages. I also found the completed ending chapter, some detailed notes, and fragments of other scenes. I decided I would finish the book for her. I read what she had written five times to get the feel of her story and writing style. I didn't want to parody her words; I wanted the words to be from the real Erin, the author. I had to discover her "voice."

When I began writing, I was astounded at the ease in which the words flowed onto the paper. The next day, I would re-read what I had written and remark, "I never wrote this!" I knew she was working though my *mind* to complete her book. Even more I felt that at times she had infused her *spirit* within my *body*.

Then, she wrote something without my fingers touching the keyboard.

As I was correcting the final draft to the manuscript, a new scene appeared on the computer display, a half a page of lines that had not been there before. Nor was it on any of the past drafts of the manuscript. The scene was on astrology, centered on the planet Venus and the divine feminine, something I know nothing about. I counted the lines—thirteen.

Erin always said thirteen was her lucky number.

One night after I completed *The Goddess Spot*, I was awakened from a deep sleep when I heard a sigh, then another sigh next to me on the side of the bed where Erin had slept. I knew it was she. Then, strangely, I heard the single flap of a wing—and she was gone. My angel had visited me. She was saying, "Thanks, my love."

I didn't expect to have another visitation, or "vision" as she would say (I had always told Erin that I wasn't good at this psychic stuff, that I couldn't clear my mind completely), but she still found a way to talk to me.

The next night in a dream, I heard these words, softly spoken, *My shining one . . .*

I stirred in my sleep, then heard, *Ireland.*

I rolled over fitfully, not yet awake, then the voice came again: *Down Cathedral.*

I tried to force myself awake as I tossed around in a bundle of sheets and covers. But the voice of Erin was gone.

I awoke the next morning, vividly remembering the dream and the words. They were burned into my memory. What was it she had said when we first met? I searched my mind, finally remembering.

The photograph haunts my mind. I know it's in Ireland. We will find that photo, the one in my vision. It is from our place in time.

In the dream she had said *Down Cathedral.* Yet, we had been there and discovered the tomb of her ancestors. Nothing more. She couldn't expect me to go back, not to Ireland. *I can't go on a fool's errand*, I thought.

Four months later, in late April, after the deep grief of her passing had softened, but not faded, I found myself in Belfast, renting a car to drive to Down Patrick. I never really thought I would find anything, but my mind would never be at ease if I didn't follow Erin's mystical words.

Through the beat of the rented car's windshield wipers I saw that the trees around Down Cathedral were no longer stark skeletons crackling in the breeze as they had been when Erin and I first visited—in what now seemed like an eternity ago.

Had it only been six months?

In the haze of a light rain I could see that the trees had started to bud and a few green leaves now unfurled. I stepped out of the car and unfolded my umbrella. Walking in the damp grass, I looked once again at the tomb of her ancestors with the rusty metal fence and the holly that masked the marble inscription.

I went in the cathedral's entryway, closed the umbrella and walked up to the granite font. I touched my fingers against the rough stone in the same spot Erin had, then dipped a finger into the water and pressed the wetness against my forehead.

"Sir, may I help you?" The voice was sharp, and I assumed I had committed a Catholic sacrilege of some kind. I wiped my finger against my pants and turned, only to be confronted by the matronly churchwoman who had helped us find the gravesite.

"Sir," she said, folding her arms below her ample boson. "I must remind you—" She stopped. She was staring into my blue eyes. Her arms fell to her side. I thought she looked ready to collapse.

With a croak in her throat, she said, "Don't I know you?"

"My wife and I, well, she . . . she died this January, we were here late last year." When the woman kept staring at me, I continued. "We were searching for my wife's ancestors. You helped us find the tomb—"

She thrust a finger toward me as if she were about to exorcise a demon from my body. "Your eyes!"

I had no answer to that.

"They're blue."

I had less of an answer to that. Perhaps *this* woman was possessed of demons, not me.

"Your wife— Oh, I am sorry for your loss. She has green eyes. She is—was—quite beautiful."

"Yes, thank you."

Then, after a long moment, she said something inexplicable. "The picture."

What!

The words began to tumble from her mouth: "After you left, I didn't know how to get hold of you, your address. I only knew you were American, but you live in such a big country, and I had no way of knowing where. I didn't even know how to locate your driver. You see, I wanted to show you—" She breathed deeply, bosom heaving.

I eased closer to her. "Show me what?"

"The picture." She swallowed hard. "And the letter."

For one brief moment, when she mentioned a picture, I thought, perhaps, just perhaps, there really was a photograph from the past, the one Erin said we would find. Then I remembered. Erin had also said, *"Maybe an old love letter will show up."*

The woman grabbed me by the arm, her fingers pinching though my sweater. "Come with me!" She practically dragged me into the room of records. The shelves of books were intact, including the huge leather-bound one she had shown us with the names of the Erin's ancestors, Robert and Margaret Smythe. Nothing had changed, not even the dry smell of dust.

She released my arm and jabbed at the drawer where I remembered the scroll with the map of cemetery lots was stored. "There!"

"The picture?" I queried, not quite sure what to do next.

"Yes, yes!" With the flat of both hands, she shooed me toward the drawer. "Open it. Go on."

The drawer creaked as it slid on the old rails. I saw nothing but the scroll.

"In the back, *under* the scroll," the woman said. "I don't know how it got there."

I reached under the scroll, hand trembling, and felt a card, which I withdrew. It looked like a letter, one that had been sewn with thread in neat stitches to a stiff card. On the front of the yellowed envelope, written in hand, was the name:

Margaret

I turned it over. On the card was a faded photograph of a man and woman. The woman was dressed in a long, full gown with bows, a flowered bonnet on her head. She was seated and the man stood next to her, hand resting on her shoulder. The photograph had been tinted in a few places: The man's wavy hair had had been colored blonde, his eyes blue, and the woman's cheeks were pink. Her eyes . . .

Her eyes had been tinted a pale *green.*

Erin, I thought, realizing the couple in the picture resembled—*us.* I felt the tears well in my eyes, and I dabbed at them with my sweater sleeve. To the woman, I said. "These are the two who are buried in the tomb?"

"I'm not sure." She backed away a few feet. "I have no idea how the picture got into the drawer. It's as if someone had left it there to be found sometime in the future."

Yes, someone had, I thought.

After a moment, I turned the photograph over. "You didn't open the letter?" I asked the woman.

"Oh my, no. 'Tis not mine to open."

"I can have it?"

"Yes, of course. It belongs to your wife."

I closed the drawer and left, holding the card and letter like it was a fragile bird.

Outside, the rain had begun to let up and I sat on a stone bench under an alcove and carefully opened the flap, fearful of tearing the fragile envelope, and slipped the letter out. I unfolded the brittle page and began to read.

My dearest Margaret,

It has now been a year since you were called to God. And it is now my time to go with him, too. I have no fear of this, as it will take me to you. You have not gone away, but continue to live inside me. You left me just as naturally as the leaves fall from the trees. Yet, you are always with me.

We will be joined together again.

I love you, Margaret.

Robert

I stared at the letter for a long time. My eyes glazed, blurring the words. Did Margaret and Robert agree to leave the photograph and letter for someone to find in the future, someone like Erin—someone like me?

Then I recalled what Erin had said about the woman being Catholic and the man, Protestant. *Like us,* she had said. *At that time the church would never allow them to marry. What if they were not destined to be together in that life because of the church? What if they made a vow to be together in another life!"*

I smiled. Margaret and Robert had found away to overcome the canons of church law and be married. Perhaps he converted to Catholicism. Yes, they were together in life, yet they had made a vow to be—I looked at the letter again—*joined together again.*

As I know Erin and I will be—somewhere in time.

I rose. I light breeze touched my face, drying my tears. I looked up and saw that the clouds had begun to clear, showing a band of sky. And I saw a rainbow, a prism of brilliant colors arching across the cobalt sky.

I remembered the words Erin had shown me, words written by author Maya Angelou:

"Each of you has the possibility of becoming rainbows for those who are yet to come."

Erin is my rainbow.

Cork Millner

Cork has written over 500 magazine articles and 15 nonfiction books, including **Hollywood Be Thy Name – The Warner Brothers Story** (which has been optioned for a Broadway musical) and a book on creative nonfiction writing titled, **Write from the Start** (Simon & Schuster). **Portraits** is a collection of twenty interviews with such celebrities as Ronald Reagan, Jimmy Stewart, Steve Martin, John Travolta, Sharon Stone and Jane Seymour. Cork's first novel, **Polo Wives,** was selected for publication by Time Warner iPublish and released in 2003. He has completed a mystery novel, **To Be or Not To Be**

Shakespeare, about a lost Shakespeare manuscript. He is the conference coordinator of the Santa Barbara Writers Conference and lives in Santa Barbara, California. He can be contacted through his website: www.corkmillner.com

Printed in the United States
35379LVS00002B/388-447